It is the height of the Roaring Twenties – a fresh enthusiasm for the arts, science, and exploration of the past have opened doors to a wider world, and beyond…

And yet, a dark shadow grows over the town of Arkham. Alien entities known as Ancient Ones lurk in the emptiness beyond space and time, writhing at the thresholds between worlds.

Occult rituals must be stopped and alien creatures destroyed before the Ancient Ones make our world their ruined dominion.

Only a handful of brave souls with inquisitive minds and the will to act stand against the horrors threatening to tear this world apart.

Will they prevail?

ALSO AVAILABLE IN ARKHAM HORROR

The Drowned City
The Forbidden Visions of Lucius Galloway by Carrie Harris
The Nightmare Quest of April May by Rosemary Jones
The Arcane Gamble of Harvey Walters by Rosemary Jones

The Adventures of Alessandra Zorzi
Wrath of N'kai by Josh Reynolds
Shadows of Pnath by Josh Reynolds
Song of Carcosa by Josh Reynolds

Visions & Nightmares, An Arkham Horror Omnibus
Also available as separate titles:
Mask of Silver by Rosemary Jones
The Deadly Grimoire by Rosemary Jones
The Bootlegger's Dance by Rosemary Jones

In the Hands of Madmen, An Arkham Horror Omnibus
Also available as separate titles:
The Last Ritual by S A Sidor
Litany of Dreams by Ari Marmell
In the Coils of the Labyrinth by David Annandale

The Ravening Deep by Tim Pratt
Herald of Ruin by Tim Pratt
The Twilight Magus by Tim Pratt

Cult of the Spider Queen by S A Sidor
Lair of the Crystal Fang by S A Sidor

The Devourer Below edited by Charlotte Llewelyn-Wells
Secrets in Scarlet edited by Charlotte Llewelyn-Wells
Dark Origins: The Collected Novellas Vol 1
Grim Investigations: The Collected Novellas Vol 2

Arkham Horror Investigators Gamebooks
The Darkness Over Arkham by Jonathan Green
The Tides of Innsmouth by Jonathan Green

Welcome to Arkham: An Illustrated Guide for Visitors
Arkham Horror: The Poster Book

THE KINGSPORT METAMORPHOSIS

JONATHAN GREEN

First published by Aconyte Books in 2026

ISBN 978 1 83908 368 6

Ebook ISBN 978 1 83908 367 9

Technical assistance by Victor Cheng

Cover art by Joshua Cairós • Book design by Nick Tyler

Interior art by Cristi Balanescu, Helge C Balzer, Yoann Boissonnet, Joshua Cairós, Adam Doyle, Rafal Hrynkiewicz, Tomasz Jedruszek, Alexander Karcz, Jacob Murray & Magali Villeneuve

Printed in the United States of America and elsewhere.

9 8 7 6 5 4 3 2 1

ACONYTE BOOKS

An imprint of Asmodee North America

Mercury House, North Gate,

Nottingham NG7 7FN, UK

aconytebooks.com

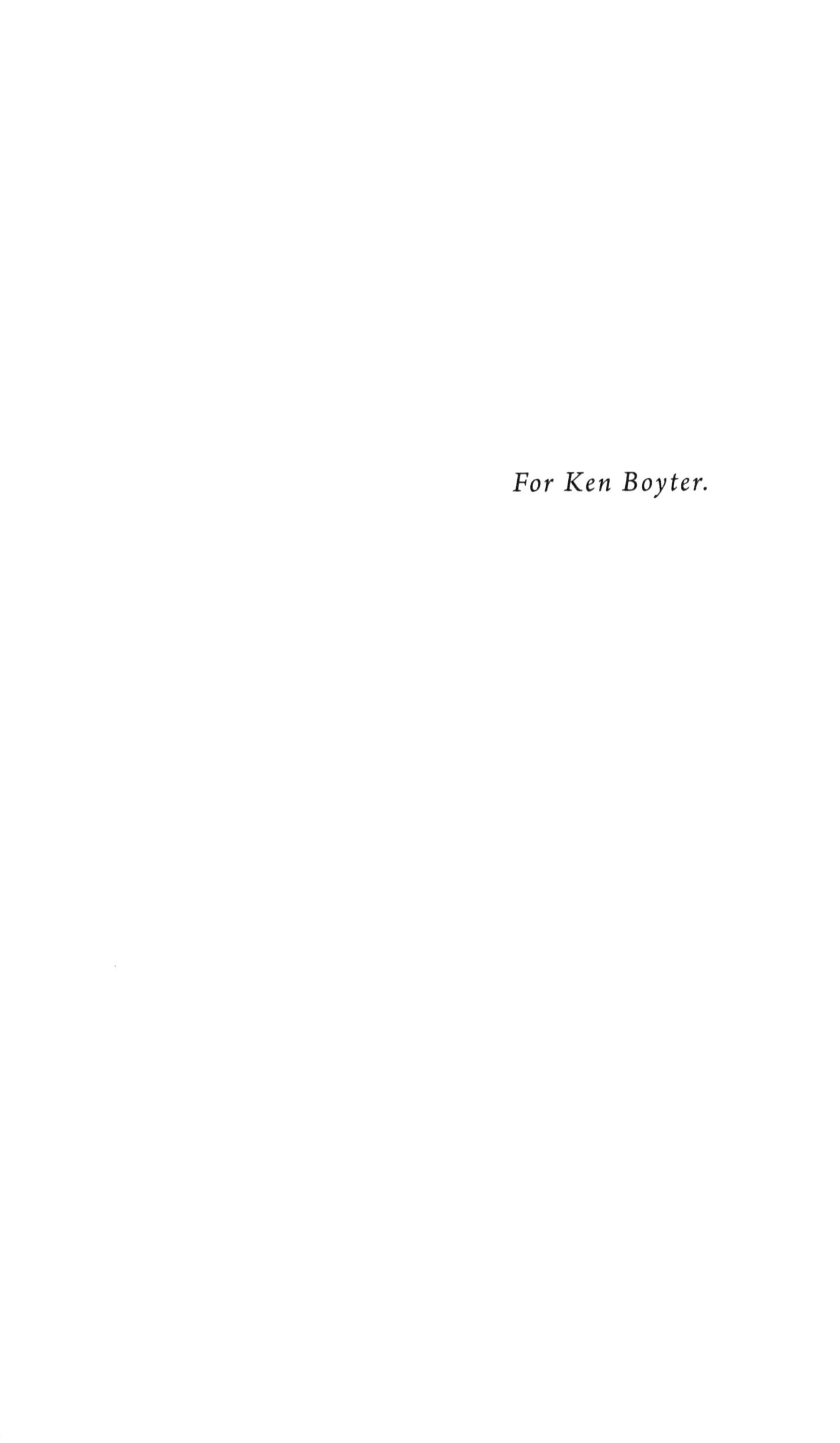

For Ken Boyter.

Greetings, Investigator.

Welcome to Kingsport.

By entering the pages of this Investigators Gamebook, you have taken on the role of one of the brave Investigators caught up in the strange goings-on at Harcourt House in the mist-shrouded New England coastal town of Kingsport.

If this is your first Investigators Gamebook, read on. If you've previously played one or more Investigators Gamebooks, turn to page **282** and read the section entitled "Continuing the Adventure" before you begin this gamebook.

A gamebook is both a book and a game. The choices you make – as well as your success in tests of **WILLPOWER**, **INTELLECT**, and **COMBAT** – will determine the route you travel through the book, deciding victory or defeat in your attempts to unravel the unfolding mystery within. If you've played other adventure gamebooks outside of the Investigators Gamebooks, you'll be familiar with the concept, but this is Kingsport, and a few things are a little… different. So, you'll want to read over the next couple of pages before your investigation begins.

Unlike most other kinds of games, you don't need to learn the rules before you start to play, but you should embrace what it means to be an Investigator to the fullest. Take note of names, locations, and anything else that might prove advantageous to you on your adventure. Some clues are obvious while others are obscure. If you're new to this type of adventure, or simply eager to begin, you have the choice to bypass some of the following instructions and leap right in. The book presents the choices you will be required to make and the tests that you will face as you go along. However, if you're curious to understand the further complexities, there are just a few things you will need before you start, and additional pointers it will prove useful to know.

WHAT YOU WILL NEED

You will need some ordinary six-sided dice – a couple is plenty. Grab them now... good work. You will also need something to keep track of your Investigator's progress. You can use the Character Sheet on page **284**, or a notepad, or piece of paper. You can also download Character Sheets from our website, https://aconytebooks.com/aconyte-extra. You'll need something to write with, and as your Investigator can both acquire and lose CLUES, RESOURCES, HEALTH, SANITY, [ITEMS], and {ABILITIES} over the course of their investigation, a pencil is ideal. Most importantly, you'll need to choose the Investigator whose role you will be playing once you begin the adventure.

CHOOSING AN INVESTIGATOR

You can find Investigator profiles for three Investigators on pages **14-17**: the psychic Jacqueline Fine, the poet Lucius Galloway, or the actress Lola Hayes. Each Investigator's profile shows all their skills, {ABILITIES}, {WEAKNESSES}, and [ITEMS], as well as their starting HEALTH and SANITY. Before you begin, you should copy these over to your Character Sheet – or simply download the pre-filled out version of the Character Sheet for your chosen Investigator from our website.

There are also some additional Investigators you'll find as

downloadable characters on our website, but if this is your first time playing through an Investigators Gamebook, we recommend using one of the three Investigators that come with this book first. Each of the Investigators featured in this gamebook has a unique introduction. However, if you choose to play as a character from a different Investigators Gamebook, or a character downloaded from the Aconyte Books website, simply start your adventure at Entry **1**. As a reminder, if you've already successfully completed an Investigators Gamebook, make sure to review the section on page **282** that tells you how to continue with your chosen Investigator.

CHARACTER SHEETS

Now that you have your Character Sheet, you are ready to begin, but first it's useful to know a little more about the information your Character Sheet presents. Your Character Sheet represents you in the role of your chosen Investigator. You are them now, and their fate is your fate. The Character Sheet tracks your progress through a number of game stats, and also provides space to record anything you pick up along the way, such as **CLUES** and **RESOURCES.**

SKILLS: WILLPOWER, INTELLECT, AND COMBAT

Each investigator has three skills: **WILLPOWER**, **INTELLECT**, and **COMBAT**. Throughout the adventure, you'll face challenges that test these skills in many different ways. When facing one of these tests, the entry in question will explain how to resolve it. Skills are represented by a number, and this number may occasionally change during the investigation.

HEALTH AND SANITY

These two game stats describe your Investigator's current physical and mental wellbeing. Like skills, they are represented by a number and tend to go down as the adventure goes on – in fact, they can even go into the negative, although they can also go up. A lower **HEALTH** or **SANITY** score will negatively impact your chances when faced with various challenges. Once these stats dip below zero, however, things will be continuously affected, and we urge you to reference your Character Sheet to account for those impacts. Try not to lose your mind, if you please.

ABILITIES AND WEAKNESSES

Abilities and Weaknesses represent special aptitudes or limitations peculiar to your chosen Investigator. Most Investigators start with a small number of each, and you may acquire other types of Abilities and Weaknesses as your investigation progresses. These Abilities and Weaknesses are represented by keywords, which don't do anything in and of themselves, but which may trigger bonuses or penalties, or other effects, depending on the challenges you encounter during the adventure. You don't need to memorize your Investigator's Abilities and Weaknesses. Instead, when an entry mentions an Ability or Weakness, you should check on your Character Sheet to see whether or not the effects described apply to you.

Sometimes, however, you may gain an Ability or Weakness as your investigation progresses. The mystery awaiting you in Kingsport is not for the faint of heart and could rattle even the most hardened Investigator, gifting you with proclivities such as {HAUNTED} or {ARACHNOPHOBIA} that don't simply fade away. Yet, great powers and abilities can also be obtained… if one has the fortitude and cleverness to earn them. These, too, for good or for ill, do not simply disappear.

Most Investigators also start with a Major Ability and a Major Weakness. You can only ever have one of each of these, and you can't lose or gain them during the course of an adventure. These Major Abilities and Major Weaknesses represent key aspects of your Investigator's personality, and each gives you a special rule, which makes playing the adventure unique to you and your character. They exist on your Investigator profile.

DOOM

The deepening mysteries and their consequences impact not just you, but the world around you. As Kingsport is beset by eldritch forces, the state of the environment shifts accordingly. **DOOM** will appear as you further unravel the mystery contained within, representing a worsening state for humanity, but a more favorable one for the creatures and Ancient Ones that have taken control of the town. Obtaining **DOOM** is most inadvisable. Try not to hand the universe over to the eldritch beings, won't you?

ITEMS

Items are exactly what you would expect: various objects your Investigator might carry with them or pick up along the way. For example, right now you have your [PENCIL] and your [SIX-SIDED DICE]. These items are keywords without any special properties, but which may prove useful in certain situations over the course of the adventure.

Most Investigators possess one starting item, representing an especially useful or cherished personal possession that can be found on their Investigator profile, which also provides you with a special rule that may prove useful at points in the adventure. These items are specific to that particular Investigator and cannot be lost, transferred, or gained.

As mentioned, other items can be found and collected during your investigation in Kingsport, but you might stumble across other items that, unless they are notated like your [PENCIL], alas, cannot be picked up. Record items you pick up on your Character Sheet but select with caution. Some items may be used to fight horrific creatures, while others might crumble the sanity you hold dear. Power corrupts, or so we're told…

CLUES AND RESOURCES

As an Investigator, you are hopefully going to uncover lots of **CLUES** along the way, as well as pick up **RESOURCES** that can help you out when things get tough. Investigators begin with **0 CLUES** and **0 RESOURCES** but can acquire them over the course of the adventure. When you acquire a **CLUE** or **RESOURCE**, add a tally mark to the relevant box on your Character Sheet. There will be times when you have the opportunity to spend a **CLUE** or **RESOURCE** to make some of the tests or puzzles you face a little easier. If you choose to do so, strike out the appropriate number of tally marks on your Character Sheet, or reference your Investigator profile for Investigator-specific abilities regarding spending **CLUES** and **RESOURCES.**

SECRETS

Lastly, as you progress you may discover SECRETS. You will find a full list of these at the end of the gamebook. When you find a SECRET, mark it off this list. You may mark off Secrets you discover across multiple playthroughs. If you're reading this in ebook format, you will have to keep track of the SECRETS you uncover elsewhere.

SUPER-SECRETS are also listed at the end of this gamebook. These are awarded for finishing the investigation with certain items in your possession, or for having marked off various SECRETS.

Remember, Kingsport is a place of cryptic mysteries – clues and secrets may be found where you least expect them, especially in any correspondence you might come across.

READY TO BEGIN?

We certainly hope so. This is not going to be easy but finding the courage to begin is the hardest part. From here on, your chances are going to be decided by the choices you make and the path you choose to follow – not to mention skill and a little luck.

This gamebook consists of individual numbered entries. Based on your choices – or your success in various tests, challenges, and puzzles – you'll be instructed to move to a specific numbered entry at the end of each step. If you're ready to begin, turn the page, read the prologue for your chosen Investigator, and good luck. The fate of mist-wreathed Kingsport, and the world as we know it, is in your hands.

Jacqueline Fine

THE PSYCHIC

 **5** WILLPOWER
 **3** INTELLECT
 **2** COMBAT
 **6** HEALTH
 **9** SANITY

STARTING ITEM

DREAM JOURNAL:
You begin each adventure with
+**1** CLUE and +**1** RESOURCE

MAJOR ABILITY

CLAIRVOYANT

For **INTELLECT** tests, you may
roll 2 dice instead of 1 and select
the dice of your choosing.

MAJOR WEAKNESS

DARK FUTURE

If you roll a double during a test,
gain +**1** DOOM and the test is
automatically unsuccessful.

OTHER ABILITIES

MYSTIC

AGILE

OTHER WEAKNESSES

TROUBLED DREAMS

PARANOIA

Lucius Galloway

THE DREAMER

2
WILLPOWER

4
INTELLECT

1
COMBAT

8
HEALTH

6
SANITY

STARTING ITEM

BOOK OF VERSE:
You may spend **RESOURCES** as if they were **CLUES** when using your **INTELLECT**.

MAJOR ABILITY

POET

Whenever you spend a **CLUE** as part of a test, if the test is successful, gain 1 **CLUE**.

MAJOR WEAKNESS

DREAMS OF THE FLOOD

Each time you gain a **CLUE**, roll 1 dice. If the number is lower than your current number of **CLUES**, do not take a **CLUE**.

OTHER ABILITIES

SEEKER
ACADEMIC
ANCIENT LANGUAGES

OTHER WEAKNESSES

TROUBLED DREAMS

Lola Hayes

The Actress

3	3	3	6	6
WILLPOWER	INTELLECT	COMBAT	HEALTH	SANITY

STARTING ITEM

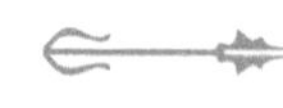

CALLING CARD:

Once per adventure, choose to gain an **ABILITY** mentioned in the entry of your choosing, if you do not already have it. You may keep this **ABILITY** for the remainder of your adventure.

MAJOR ABILITY

IMPROVISATION

Once per adventure, you may increase a skill of your choice by +**1** but you must also decrease a skill by -**1**. You may use this ability more than once per adventure, but after the first time, you must spend +**1 RESOURCE** for each additional use.

OTHER ABILITIES

GUARDIAN

QUICK-WITTED

MAJOR WEAKNESS

CRISIS OF IDENTITY

Each time you spend a **RESOURCE**, roll 1 dice. If you roll a 1, lose **1** SANITY.

OTHER WEAKNESSES

HAUNTED

CURSED

CAUTIOUS

The mists of Kingsport are nothing new to you. Ever since you were a child you have felt their smothering, oppressive presence pressing on your mind and carried within them are voices from places you cannot name.

Some may dismiss you as flighty and fanciful, but you know the truth of what you hear – whispers that drift across the threshold of dreams, fragments of futures yet to pass, warnings of dangers stirring the unseen world.

For years you tried to quiet these unnatural revelations, to bury them beneath the banality of routine and reason, but they would always return with relentless persistence. Now you have learned to heed them, using their cryptic guidance to navigate through the world and the secret threats that lie hidden beneath the surface of reality, even when it brings you to places most would avoid.

So, when your supernatural senses pull you toward the mist-bound streets of Kingsport with a peculiar letter in your hand, you understand that you have no choice but to follow where they lead.

Now turn to **1**.

Words have always come easily to you, but sleep does not – not since your partner Rudi disappeared. And when sleep does come, your dreams are haunted by visions of the same hazy underwater city, night after night. It is this place that you capture within your poetry, hoping that by writing about the impossible sunken city you might understand it and discover what has happened to Rudi.

Your publishers hail you as a visionary, your critics as a madman. You are no longer sure which claim is closer to the truth. What you do know is that the mists of Kingsport haunted your work long before you set foot in the town. Your notebooks are filled with mist-wreathed streets, winding stairways, and faces glimpsed only in the unreal world of your dreams, such as they are.

And now that you walk the alleyways of Kingsport, summoned by the curious letter tucked into your jacket pocket, if the truth of your visions await you here, you will meet them, whether it brings triumph or ruin.

Now turn to **1**.

LOLA

As an accomplished actress, you can transform yourself into anyone – the dutiful daughter, the tragic lover, the queen betrayed. The roles change but the mask never falters. Yet after the stage lights have dimmed and the applause of the audience is no more than a remembered echo, you have begun to wonder how much of yourself remains once the curtain falls.

You first encountered the name Kingsport not in a script but in an overheard whisper, spoken on stage by an actor who had no recollection afterward of doing so. Since then, the town has haunted your thoughts. So, when a letter arrives from one Elijah Harcourt inviting you to visit his home in Kingsport, you decide it might be nice to have a break from performing and distract yourself with whatever awaits you in the misty seaside town.

But, as you come to the coast, you can't help wondering if perhaps you are about to take on the most important role of your life.

> Now turn to **1**.

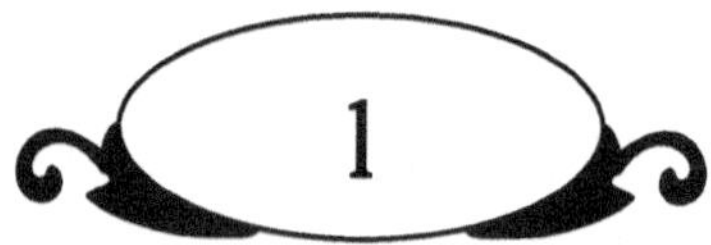

The town of Kingsport sits at the mouth of the Miskatonic River, where the water empties into the Atlantic Ocean, bracketed by the scenic cliffs that ring the bay below. Most impressive of these cliffs is Kingsport Head, a large, rocky peninsula connected to the mainland by a long causeway. The cliffs, like the seaside destination of South Shore and the Kingsport Caverns, draw visitors from all over New England. But you are not here to see the sights.

Something else that Kingsport is famous for are the mists. Those of a logical and scientific bent assert that the cliffs create a geological feature – a vast, natural bowl – that traps the moist air required for the low-lying clouds to form. Others, of a much more fanciful disposition, imagine the mists to have some impossible, otherworldly origin. What is an indisputable fact, however, is that the slow, swirling sea fogs are certainly sluggish when it comes to leaving the town's streets, and there are many local legends associated with them. But it is not the mists, or these legends, that have brought you here on this day, either.

Arriving in town, you take a moment to consider the forbidding sharp rise of Kingsport Head and the coiling mists lingering within the town's streets and alleyways, to reflect on what has really brought you to this place at this time.

You take the letter from your pocket and read it for the umpteenth time. It is addressed to you personally and has been written in a looping, spidery hand:

I trust this letter finds you in sound mind and good health, for what I must impart will require both.

Though we have not met – nor, I suspect, have you heard my name – I have followed your pursuits with great interest and a sense of inevitable convergence. Circumstances most peculiar and urgent compel me to request your presence at Harcourt House, on the cliffs overlooking the South Shore of Kingsport. You will arrive, I hope, during the autumnal equinox, at precisely seven o'clock in the evening.

As I approach my sixth decade, and though the years have taken their toll upon me, it is not age that troubles me now. It is memory… and the return of things I had long thought buried. Matters long dormant now stir in the darkness, and I fear they are not content to remain in the shadows any longer. I believe you, of all people, possess the necessary faculties to comprehend – and perhaps confront – what must soon be brought into the light.

This invitation is not extended lightly. Come alone.

Bring no companion. Tell no one. What I reveal must remain unspoken to the uninitiated, lest they, too, fall prey to what lies beyond the borders of this world.
We will meet at my home at the allotted hour.
In utmost confidence,
Elijah Harcourt

Considering you have no idea who Elijah Harcourt is, or why he wants your help, and having several hours to while away before you are expected at Harcourt House, you decide to spend the time wisely. You want to see what you can find out about the man before you meet him for the first time. But where do you want to search for information?

The Central Hill neighborhood of Kingsport is where a visitor will find buildings richly steeped in history with some of them dating from the Revolutionary era, if not before. While the wealthy elite of the town are wary of strangers turning up at their doorstep unannounced, it is here that one could connect with the numerous working-class people who break their backs for Kingsport's wealthy citizens, and who might be willing to share what goes on behind the closed doors lining Central Hill.

Kingsport's Harborside is an example of the quintessential New England docks and is where the mists that plague the town are thickest. Several drinking establishments can be found among the weatherworn warehouses that proliferate in this area. They are frequented by itinerant sailors as well as the local dockworkers, and are doubtless a hotbed of gossip.

The South Shore community, on the other hand, is where you will find the arts and entertainment district. The boardwalk has an electric carousel, as well as games and food stands, but it is also where you will find wandering psychics, mediums and clairvoyants – the kind who will tell your fortune if you cross their palm with silver.

So, which part of town do you want to visit before you are due at Harcourt House?

Central Hill: turn to **51**.
Harborside: turn to **131**.
South Shore: turn to **211**.

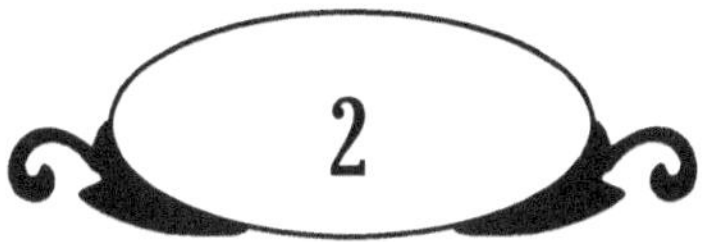

2

There are many stories about those who have lost their way within the mist-bound streets of Kingsport, and not all of them have a happy ending. You wouldn't want to become one of them, would you?

If you are reading this because you finished the first section and simply kept on going, we must warn you that you are going to get confused very quickly, which is sure to take its toll on your sanity. This book only makes sense if you hop from entry to entry, according to the choices you make and the directions you're given. We suggest you go back to Entry 1 and choose one of the options listed there, then turn to the appropriate entry.

However, maybe you're here because you think this section is the solution to one of the puzzles in the book. It isn't. Whoever said that solving the mystery locked within Harcourt House was going to be easy? However, we'll let you award yourself a Secret on this occasion. Take SECRET: *Seeker After Truth.*

Then again, perhaps you're here because you are actively scouring the book for Secrets. Not a bad tactic, and this time it's scored you a prize. Take SECRET: *Secrets and Lies.*

And then again, maybe you've undertaken such an adventure before and learned that turning to Entry **2** is a sure way to win yourself some SECRETS, and it has worked again. Take SECRET: *Underhanded.*

Now go back to whatever it was you were doing before, which may well mean returning to Entry **1**.

3

At long last, the glow of lamps in the windows of a house become distinct orbs of light through the mist, and the crunch of gravel resumes under your feet. You have found sanctuary at last. You are exhausted and hungry, and at your wits' end, but at least now you are safe.

You quicken your steps as relief floods through you, and the shape of the house emerges. You see the steps leading up to a dark front door, and a familiar arrangement of windows and roof ridges. A chill knot of terror, colder than the cloying mist, seizes hold of your stomach and twists.

Somehow you have found your way back to Harcourt House.

Resigned, you climb the steps once more, push open the front door, and stagger to the parlor where you collapse into a chair. Take -**1 HEALTH** and +**1 DOOM**.

Peregrine Ward and Horace Trenholm are having a heated discussion, but break off when they hear Isabel Harcourt exclaim, "What happened to you?"

"I got lost in the mist," you say weakly.

"What are you talking about?" she counters. "You've only been gone five minutes – ten at most – just enough time to walk to the end of the drive and back, I imagine. And what have you been up to, to end up in such a state and in such a short time?"

Five minutes? But you've been gone hours. Is she trying to pull one over on you?

You heave yourself out of your seat and make your way back into the front hall to check the time on the grandfather clock. Unless her ruse has stretched to resetting the clock, it's clear that you've been gone hardly any time at all. So, what happened to you out there in the mists?

Take -2 **SANITY**, and the SECRET: *Grim Villas* in the Mist.

Turn to **175**.

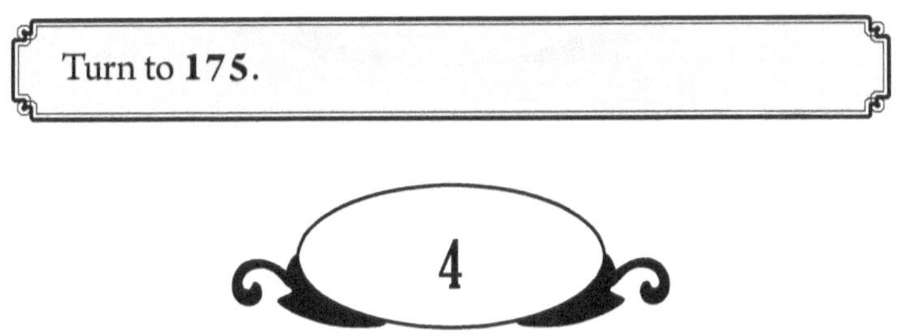

4

Getting down on your hands and knees, you pull up the corner of the valance and peer into the darkness that has collected beneath the four-poster.

As your eyes adjust to the gloom you begin to make out myriad glistening orbs that shine like polished black pearls in the low light now penetrating the shadows under the bed. There must be hundreds of them!

It takes a moment longer for your eyesight to adjust enough for you to realize that what you are looking at are hundreds of eyes, belonging to dozens of spiders of varying sizes. Some are clinging to the bed frame while others are squatting on the carpet amidst the balls of dust and hair and look like they could spring at any moment.

You let the valance drop and quickly get to your feet, backing away from the bed toward the door, watching the floor for any sign that the spiders have chosen to follow you.

Take **-1 SANITY**, **+1 DOOM**, and gain the Weakness **{ARACHNOPHOBIA}**, if you don't have it already.

If you have some [**PINCE-NEZ GLASSES**],
turn to **48.**
If not, turn to **170.**

5

You hesitate, and in that instant, Peregrine Ward snatches the letter from you. Take **-1 WILLPOWER**.

"I would ask you to maintain an appropriate level of decorum while we try to work out what is going on," the attorney says, addressing you and Trenholm together. He slips the letter into the breast pocket of his gray jacket.

"You think there's something going on?" the explorer says. "You don't think what happened to Elijah and Cora was an accident?"

"Do you?" bites back Ward.

A strange look passes between the two of them, but what does it mean? Clearly, they know something you don't.

"If one of us was to read the letter, maybe we would learn the truth," says Trenholm.

Turn to **166.**

6

The spider makes its getaway, vanishing into a darkened corner of the study and leaving you with the unwelcome knowledge that it is still loose. Now, anyone could become its next victim.

You suddenly find yourself imagining a host of spiders scuttling over the floor toward you and you take a step back, only for your imaginary arachnids to start descending the walls on either side of the study door. You shudder and stifle a moan of revulsion. Take -**1 SANITY**.

Someone suddenly cries, "Look out!" – you don't know who – and the group scatters. There is some commotion within the study and then Horace Trenholm abruptly exits the room, holding a glass jar in his hand, with its lid screwed down tight, and a large spider trapped inside.

Its bulbous black body is covered with strange, skull-like scarlet Rorschach inkblot markings, while the creature's eyes are myriad gleaming black pearls. Then, there are the overlarge mandibles, a droplet of clear liquid collecting at the tip of each needle-like fang. With its legs extended, it would be as big across as your balled fist.

Turn to **244.**

It seems like every hour you make another unpleasant discovery in this horrible house of spiders!

Where do you want to go now?

> To investigate Harcourt's so-called "Museum," turn to **38**.
>
> To return to the bookcase-door and see what lies behind it, turn to **188**.
>
> To go downstairs and inform the others of what has happened, turn to **233**.

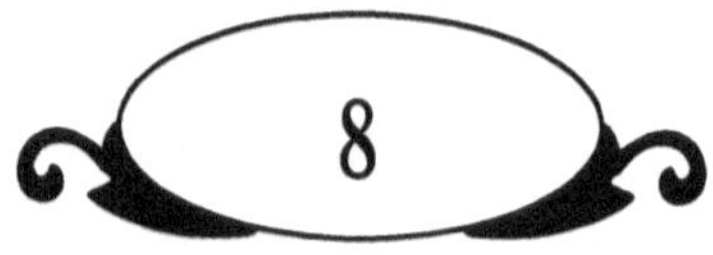

Upon entering the bedchamber, you find that there is nobody there. The four-poster bed shows signs of having been slept in, but Elijah Harcourt isn't here now.

Was he well enough to walk out of the bedroom of his own will and volition, or has he been moved somewhere else? If it is the former, where is he now? If it is the latter, who moved him, where have they moved him to, and why? Take +**2 DOOM**.

> If you want to search the room for clues, turn to **28**.
> If you want to leave the room immediately, to look for the missing invalid, turn to **48**.

9

Turning on the [FLASHLIGHT], you point it at the nearest of the advancing horrors. As the bright beam strafes across its eyes, the thing gives a hiss and scampers back a few steps. Others continue to approach from the darkness, but as you turn the [FLASHLIGHT] on them, they also hiss and back away.

In this way, you retreat back toward the house. However, having spent so long in close proximity to the overgrown spider-things, you feel shaken to the very core. Not only that, but your sojourn into the grounds has left you with filthy footwear. Take -1 SANITY and record your [DIRTY SHOES] on your Character Sheet, if you haven't done so already.

You finally make it back to the steps up to the front door, the creatures having quit stalking you some time ago, and opening the door, let yourself back inside.

Turn to **282**.

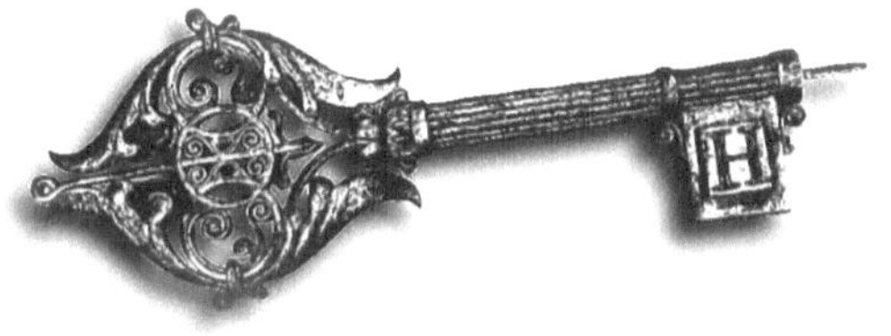

Catching a glimpse of a figure darting around upstairs, you investigate. Peering up from the hall to the second floor landing above, you see one of the housemaids – unmistakable in her black dress and white apron, her russet hair tied in a bun and covered by a mob cap – peer back down over the banister.

Make an entropy test. Roll one die, and if you have the Weakness {**PARANOID**} or {**TROUBLED DREAMS**}, deduct 1.

If the result is equal to or lower than the current **DOOM** level, turn to **212**.

If not, turn to **202**.

Having read the letter, you turn it over and make out the shadowed impressions left by Harcourt's pen. The piece of paper on which he wrote your letter must have been underneath another sheet upon which he was composing a missive to someone else.

Angling the paper so that it catches the light the right way, you are able to make out what at least part of the letter says.

one last service, greater than the first, and far more

binding. Its nature I shall not reveal in this letter; ink and paper are too frail a bulwark against prying eyes.

When next we commune, you will have already taken up the role

Take + **1 CLUE** and the *Secret: Hidden Two*.

> Turn back to **216**.

12

The mist hugs the house, smothering it in its chill embrace. Descending the steps, you warily set off down the drive. The fog is so thick you can barely make out the trees to either side of you, even though you know they are only a few feet away at most.

Turning, you look back at the house, but all you can see is the suffused glow of the porch light and the lit lamps inside the rooms where the curtains or shutters have not yet been closed. However, you are sure you won't get lost and so set off again down the drive.

Making it to the gates, you can see no sign of any vehicle approaching the house along the road – not that you can see the road! You don't think there is anything to be gained by leaving the grounds, seeing as how the mist is so all-encompassing, and so you turn around and walk back along the drive between the red maples. Upon reaching the house, you climb the steps and let yourself in.

Isabel Harcourt, Peregrine Ward and Horace Trenholm are

all standing in a huddle in the middle of the front hall in deep, anxious discussion. However, as you enter the house all eyes fixate on you.

"Where have you been?" Isabel exclaims, unable to hide her agitation.

"What do you mean?" you ask.

"You've been gone almost an hour."

"What? No, I haven't. I went down the drive to the gates and back. I can't have been more than ten minutes."

At that moment, the grandfather clock in the hall chimes the hour, making you a liar.

"Look at the state of your shoes," Ward says, pointing. "You claim you went down the drive, but it looks like you've been walking through a muddy field."

You look down and see for yourself how filthy your footwear is, but you can't explain why. Cold shock seizes your body.

Take -1 **SANITY** and record the fact that you have [**DIRTY SHOES**] on your Character Sheet.

Turn to **162**.

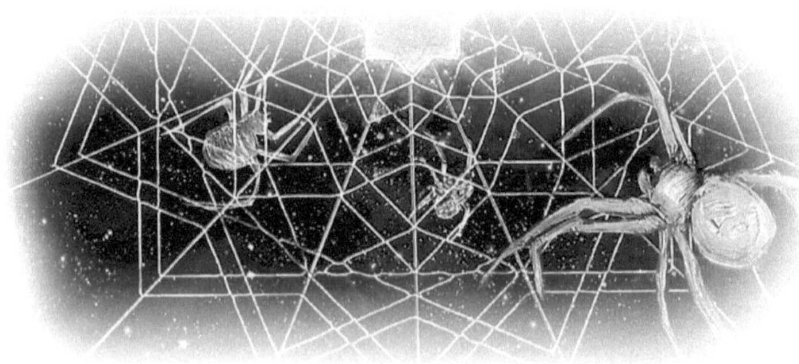

Forgotten Cults of Hyperborea is a crumbling folio whose introduction claims it contains information gained from translating fragments of pre-human stone tablets and the lost records of the mad magus Eibon of Mhu-Thulan. It concerns the secret societies, dark heresies, and nightmare religions that proliferated within Hyperborea – that legendary, ice-haunted continent long sunk beneath the seas and preserved now only in myth.

The sects and societies listed within include the Cult of Tsathoggua, devoted to the bloated god of sloth; the snake-worshippers of Yig, the father of serpents; the frostbound sorcerers, and the children of Atlach-Nacha. It is this last one that catches your attention in particular.

Devotees of the spider goddess seemed to believe that she dwelt in caverns deep beneath Hyperborea, weaving a colossal, never-ending web that stretched across realities with each new strand forming a bridge between worlds. Neophytes were entombed in darkness, kept alive until spiders consumed their flesh, with any survivors being considered marked by Atlach-Nacha to become her children. To the cult, the impossible web was destiny itself, and all beings were trapped within its strands. To serve the spinner in darkness was to accept and embrace one's place in the design.

Take +**1 CLUE**, and if you want to take the book with you, record [**FORGOTTEN CULTS OF HYPERBOREA**] on your Character Sheet and take the Ability {**ARCANE STUDIES**}.

Turn to **110.**

14

The books seem to be a mix of travelogues, treatises about long forgotten pagan practices, and encyclopedias of the natural world. They have evocative and intriguing titles, such as *7 Months up the Amazon*, *6 Sects of the Sierra de Arañas*, and *A Naturalist's Guide to the Spiders of Borneo*, which is an introductory identification guide to the 280 most commonly seen species.

Turn to **289**.

15

As more spiders drop onto you from above, what do you want to bring to bear against the swarm?

Choose one of the items on your Character Sheet and then turn to **138**.

Everything is just as you left it. In fact, you're not really sure why you have bothered to return here. The map on the wall above the camp-bed, with its fantastical illustrations and placenames that sound like something someone dreamt up whilst in a fugue state, unsettles you. It's like somewhere you've visited before, but never while you were awake.

In fact, you feel uneasy just being here. Take **- 1 SANITY**.

If you want to leave the secret room, hoping the feelings of unease will then pass, turn to **258**.
If you want to open the cupboard, turn to **286**.

Crossing the hall, you enter the study to find Peregrine Ward crouched in front of the fireplace. The smell of burning catches in your nostrils, startling you. The fire wasn't lit in the room previously, so what can be burning now?

You in turn startle Ward, who rises and walks for the door, acting as if you don't exist. He refuses to make eye contact, his body strung taut as a wire. But you hold your ground and stand in his way.

Everything about this situation and his behavior suggests to you that he's up to no good. Instinctively, you prepare to stop him. But Peregrine Ward isn't going to let anyone stand in his way.

Make a resistance test. Roll one die and add your **COMBAT**. You may spend **1 RESOURCE** to roll two dice and pick the highest. If you have the {FIGHTER}, {GUARDIAN}, {RESOLVED}, {ROGUE}, or {TOUGH} Ability, add 1. If you have the Weakness {CAUTIOUS}, deduct 1. What's the result?

Total of 8 or more: turn to **222**.
7 or less: turn to **122**.

You push into the webbed portal, its strands thick as rope, clinging to your skin with a damp, living resistance. Horribly, they feel like strands of muscle – warm, pulsing, and somehow aware. The air grows heavy with a sour-sweet musk, the scent of ancient decay and spun silk. Isabel hesitates behind you, but there's no turning back now.

As you force your way through, you fall, sliding down a slope of webbing that trembles under your weight. You land hard at the bottom of the vast cavern, its ceiling lost in shadow. Webs crisscross the space, glistening with threads that hum faintly, as if resonating with some unheard song.

Shapes scuttle in the gloom – spiders, yes, but like nothing on Earth. Hulking, many-eyed, their bodies glistening. But they don't charge, they only watch.

At the far end of the chamber, a vast shape stirs. You feel it before you see it: the weight of a god, impossibly still, impossibly vast. Eight eyes flick open, and the great spinner unfolds from her webbed throne.

You have entered the lair of Atlach-Nacha, the spider queen. There can be no escape for you now.

Take the SECRET: *The Spider and the Fly.*

The End.

Leaving the mysterious map room, you close the bookcase-door behind you, your mind full of questions.

Where do you want to go now?

> If you want to investigate Harcourt's so-called "Museum," turn to **38.**
>
> If you want to check on Elijah Harcourt, turn to **88.**
>
> If you want to go downstairs and inform the others of what has happened, turn to **233.**

Having distributed the letters, Knott still has one left. "Dr Cora Bellweather," he says, reading out the name on the envelope.

"Where is Dr Bellweather?" Ward asks, his tone irritated.

It is at that moment that you hear a cry from across the hall, followed by the sound of something hitting the floor.

Ward leads the way across the hall at a trot before coming to an abrupt halt at the entrance to the study. The double doors remain open, no one having closed them when they left because Dr Bellweather was still in the room. And she is still in the room, only now she is lying on the floor. Her eyes are closed but she is groaning as if in pain, and a sheen of sweat can be seen on her brow.

"Looks like she found the spider," says Trenholm, pointing. "Look at her hand."

The back of her right hand is livid purple and is already starting to swell as the spider's venom takes effect.

Dr Harrow is about to enter the study when Professor Varnum puts out an arm to stop him. "Don't go in there," he hisses.

"I have to!" Harrow counters.

"But the spider is clearly still on the loose in there."

"It is my duty. I swore an oath."

While the two men are busy arguing, a desperate urge comes over you to do something. But what?

To go to Dr Bellweather's aid, turn to **98**.

To enter the study specifically to find the spider, turn to **128**.

To stay where you are, as recommended by Otto Varnum, turn to **158**.

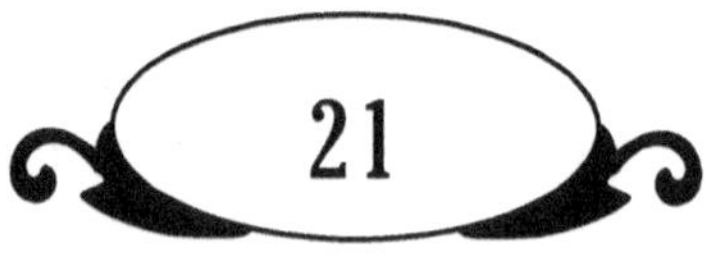

21

Fearing that the desperate doctor might try to stab you or Harcourt with the hypodermic needle and inject who knows what into your veins, you charge him, determined to subdue him before he can act.

You may spend **1 RESOURCE** at the start of each round to add 2 to your total for that round.

Round one: roll two dice and add your **COMBAT**. If you have the {AGILE} or {SURVIVOR} Ability, add 1. If you have the Weakness {CAUTIOUS}, deduct 1. If the total is 14 or more, you win the first round.

Round two: roll two dice and add your **COMBAT** and your **WILLPOWER**. If you have the {FIGHTER} or {TOUGH} Ability, add 1. If you won the first round, add 2. If your total is 15 or more, you win the second round.

> If you won the second round, turn to **36**.
> If you lost the second round, turn to **56**.

22

Outside, there is no sign of the explorer – you cannot even hear his howls of terror or the crunch of gravel under his flying feet. Everything is muffled by the mists.

> If you want to persist in trying to track down Trenholm, turn to **102**.
> If you would rather steel your resolve and return to the house to discover Ward's fate, turn to **288**.

You assist Trenholm and Dr Harrow in carefully carrying the unconscious man from the study, turning left upon entering the hall, and carry him upstairs. The staircase curves around the west wall of the hall to the second-floor landing. Dr Harrow leads the way, clearly having ministered to Elijah Harcourt at home before, for he knows where his bedroom is located.

You circle the landing, passing doors to several other rooms, including one on the north side of the landing bearing the sign "Museum," until you are directly above where you began to climb the staircase. Passing through a small vestibule, you enter Harcourt's bedchamber. The bed itself is a solidly built mahogany four-poster. Its gauzy covering puts you in mind of thick swathes of cobwebs. Heavy drapes are drawn across the windows, but the household servants have already turned down the covers and left a bedside lamp switched on.

Once you and Trenholm have laid Elijah Harcourt on the bed, Dr Harrow dismisses you. "Return to the others. I will carry out a proper examination and join you downstairs when I am done."

"I can't believe something as innocuous as a spider bite could do that to a man," you say to Trenholm in an effort to make small talk as the two of you descend the stairs once again to rejoin the others.

"He's lucky we're in North America and not South America," says the explorer. "I was once with a man when he was bitten by a Brazilian wandering spider in the Amazon. He was dead within half an hour, but he begged me to kill him long before that. It was the pain, you see."

"It's not even been fifteen minutes since Harcourt was bitten," you point out. "Do you think that might happen to Harcourt?"

"It would help us understand the effects of its venom, at least, and maybe even identify the spider," Trenholm agrees with a grim smile. "However, I doubt anything from South America could live long in Kingsport, especially with the cold weather. How would such a creature survive the journey to Massachusetts in the first place and then manage to survive Harcourt's cold office? But spiders are intrepid creatures, able to survive conditions I wouldn't expect, and I am no zoologist."

The explorer has done nothing to put your mind at ease. In fact, you find yourself shooting anxious glances at the darkened corners of the front hall, wondering if the eight-legged horror that attacked Harcourt is hiding somewhere in the shadows.

Take -1 **SANITY** and the SECRET: *Creepy-Crawly.*

Turn to **173**.

24

Having rid yourself of the spiders, and while Isabel continues to battle to keep the arachnids at bay, you redouble your efforts to rouse the sleepers and break their connection to the domain of the spinner in darkness.

Grabbing Dr Luther Harrow by the shoulders, you shake him violently while screaming in his face to wake up. His eyelids suddenly flick open, and he meets your gaze with a terrified stare. His eyes seeming to bulge out of his head, and opening his mouth, he utters a high-pitched, bloodcurdling scream.

The scream is taken up by the other sleepers, who are also waking to the uncomfortable truth of the situation in which they now find themselves. And then the spider-thing squatting in the middle of the massive web starts to scream too, and you fear that your mind will break.

Roll one die.

> If the number rolled is equal to or less than your **SANITY**, turn to **176**.
> If the number rolled is greater than your **SANITY**, turn to **159**.

Being surrounded by so many artifacts connected to spider cults the world over makes you feel uneasy, as if the web of devotees to the eight-legged goddess has snared the entire planet.

Take - **1 SANITY** and the SECRET: *World Wide Web.*

What do you want to do now?

To take a look at the framed drawing, turn to **73**.
To examine the collection of photographs, turn to **224**.
To leave the museum and look elsewhere, turn to **170**.

Overcome by the horror and mind-wrenching impossibility of everything that is assailing your senses, you find yourself frozen to the spot and unable to resist as the Harcourt-spider climbs down from its web and crosses the dusty floorboards. Its strange eight legs look like wrongly jointed human arms that then meld into a claw-tipped and bristled spider leg, but nonetheless allow the creature to scuttle in a grotesque walk across the attic.

"Behold the Key!" you hear the butler cry out. "Flesh-bound, dream-marked, woven in shadow and chosen to fulfil this great purpose. The Key is true."

The creature that was once Elijah Harcourt looms over you, a human face melded in a sickening metamorphosis to the swollen spider-body, mouth distended, fangs twitching.

"And now the Key must turn!" comes Knott's voice again.

It is the last thing you ever hear as, with a sudden crunch of bone and a splash of warmth, your head is cleanly severed from your body by the monster's jaws.

The End.

Breaking free of the ring of spiders, you sprint toward the house, not once daring to look back. If they are coming after you, intending on finishing you off, you would rather not know about it. Sometimes, ignorance really is bliss.

But even when you are back inside the house, with the door closed and bolted against the horrors that are lurking within the grounds, knowing what is waiting for anyone foolhardy enough to step outside leaves you in a state of high agitation.

Make a note on your Character Sheet that you have [DIRTY SHOES], if you haven't done so already, and if you do not have them already, gain the Weaknesses {ARACHNOPHOBIA} and {HAUNTED}.

Turn to **282.**

The décor feels dated, like something out of the previous century. As well as the bed, there are three other notable pieces of furniture in Harcourt's bedroom – a bedside table, a tallboy, and a three-door French oak armoire.

Where do you want to focus your search, at least to begin with?

The bedside table: turn to **167**.
The tallboy: turn to **187**.
The armoire: turn to **207**.
Under the bed: turn to **4**.

Neither of you look back once as you run down the attic stairs, taking them two at a time. Reaching the second-floor landing, you race for the central staircase and upon reaching the front hall again, throw open the door and head out into the night.

But the pernicious mist that has surrounded Harcourt House since you arrived appears to be dissipating at last. You and Isabel run down the drive, through the gates, and away along the road toward the town that lies below the cliffs.

Elijah Harcourt is dead, but the house full of dreams and spiders still stands. And who knows what kind of fate you have doomed the other guests to…

SECRET: *Oh, What A Tangled Web.*

Final score: 2 stars.

The End.

The optical illusion is starting to give you a headache. You have the inkling that you won't feel better until you have quit this gloomy room. Perhaps it is the preponderance of potent artifacts all contained within one place, but you feel compelled to leave the oppressive museum before you have a complete mental breakdown.

Take -**1 HEALTH** and -**1 WILLPOWER**.

> Turn to **170**.

"Oh yes," replies the academic, "years."

"So, you're close," you add.

"We were once, but not now." A wistful look enters his eyes.

"Can I ask why?"

The professor hesitates before replying. "We had a difference of opinion."

"What sort of difference of opinion?"

Varnum gives a heartfelt sigh. "Elijah wanted to take our mutual studies to the next stage. I didn't."

"What do you mean by 'the next stage'?" you ask.

"To move from the hypothetical to the practical. He wanted to take the step from academic study to actual reenactment."

"And you disagreed."

"I most certainly did. While I may have an interest in the occult, I am not interested in practicing black magic."

Take +**1 CLUE**.

Turn to **129**.

32

The mist seems as thick yet light as cotton candy, and with every breath you take you feel its chill dampness at the back of your throat.

If you have a [**SHIRT BUTTON**], turn to **125**.

If not, but you have some [**PINCE-NEZ GLASSES**], turn to **102**.

If not, but you have a [**FOSSIL FANG**], turn to **66**.

If you do not have any of the above items, turn to **12**.

33

If Knott has worked for Harcourt for thirty-three years, there cannot be very much that he doesn't know about his employer, or his obsessions. And knowing that – plus the way he stares adoringly at the webs – tells you something about the state of his mind that kindles a vital spark of hope in yours.

Take +1 **SANITY**, +1 **WILLPOWER**, and the Secret: *Hidden Five.*

Now turn back to **92.**

34

There are numerous different sized jars and bottles, containing all manner of spiders. Some have great, long legs like a spider crab, while others are minuscule, little more than glistening black beads with pin-like limbs. There are even some that look like large bird-eating spiders, covered in coarse hair.

If you have the Weakness {**ARACHNOPHOBIA**}, take -1 **WILLPOWER**.

Fortunately, all the specimens are long dead and are suspended now in some kind of embalming fluid that prevents them from decaying.

Turn to **289.**

Leaping forward, you slam the pot down on top of the spider – only your reflexes aren't quite sharp enough and you miss by a hair's breadth. Still, it is enough that the spider escapes. Take -1 **COMBAT**, +1 **DOOM**, and the SECRET: *The One That Got Away.*

"Give me that!" Horace Trenholm barks, snatching the container from you. Strike the [EMPTY GLASS JAR] from your Character Sheet.

Without pausing, he throws himself after the running spider, landing flat on his stomach on the floor. It is only when he gets up again that you see he has the hideous horror trapped inside the glass container and the lid screwed down tight.

Its bulbous black body is covered with strange, skull-like scarlet Rorschach inkblot markings, while its eyes are myriad gleaming black pearls. Then, there are the overlarge mandibles, a droplet of clear liquid collecting at the tip of each needle-like fang. With its legs extended, it would be as big across as your balled fist.

Turn to **244**.

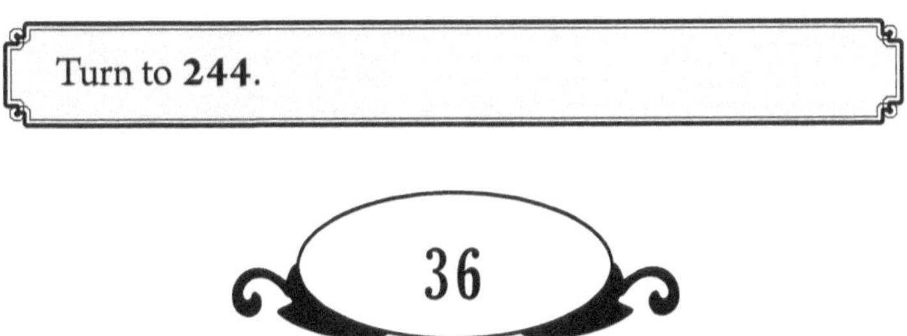

You wrestle the syringe from the doctor's grasp and with a heartfelt sigh of resignation he sits down suddenly on the edge of the bed.

"I wasn't going to harm Elijah," he says in a quiet voice. "It was for me."

"Excuse me?" You stare from the doctor to the hypodermic needle now in your hand and back again.

Then, his confession pours out of him: "A patient of mine died. Elijah could tell something was wrong and, in a moment of rash despair, I confided in him. He said he would deal with the matter and that I wasn't to worry. And he did deal with it, or rather he instructed Peregrine Ward to make the problem go away. For a blissful time, it was gone. I didn't have to worry. But from that moment on, Elijah Harcourt as good as owned me. The opioids make me forget all the things I've done."

Take + **1 CLUE** and the SECRET: *An Apple a Day.*

Turn to **182.**

37

Flailing at the scuttling bodies, you fight to brush them off as quickly as you can, hoping that none of them bite you as a result.

Round one: roll two dice and add your **COMBAT**. If you have the {AGILE}, {RESOLVED} or {SURVIVOR} Ability, add 1. If you have the Weakness {CAUTIOUS}, deduct 1. If the total is 14 or more, you win the first round.

Round two: roll two dice and add your **COMBAT** and your **WILLPOWER**. If you have the {FIGHTER} or

{TOUGH} Ability, add 1. If you won the first round, add 2. If your total is 15 or more, you win the second round.

If you won the second round, turn to **78**.
If you lost the second round, turn to **49**.

38

You are surprised to find Horace Trenholm in the museum, standing in front of a glass display case that contains Elijah Harcourt's most rare and unusual treasures. Blinds are drawn down over the windows, and the room is illuminated by a handful of electric lights. Reflected in the glass, Trenholm's features have an unhealthy yellow cast to them that only serves to highlight the areas that are in shadow, such as his eyes and the hollow of his cheeks. In fact, it makes his face look a lot like a skull.

Sensing your presence, he tries to hide the battered stainless steel hip flask he is holding before thinking better of it.

"As I thought," he says, indicating the cabinet. Inside, you make out a curved stone spike, just like the one now in your possession, resting on a velvet cushion. Next to it is an impression in the cushion where its twin must have lain. "This is where they got the murder weapon."

"Professor Varnum is still alive," you point out.

"For the time being," Trenholm replies.

"But you believe this once belonged to a spider?" you say, holding up the [FOSSIL FANG].

"That's what Cora said." His voice is strangely distant. "You should have seen some of the things he paid her to acquire for him. Nothing with fangs like these, of course, but big enough. Too big if you ask me. No one was the wiser, despite my worries. But as long as he kept funding her work, she kept bringing him what he wanted."

You recognize the look in his eyes. Fear.

Finding Trenholm in such a talkative mood, you decide to probe the explorer for more information. But what do you want to ask him?

"What did Harcourt need the spiders for?" Turn to **67**.

"What did Harcourt pay you to do?" Turn to **97**.

"What was in Harcourt's letter to you?" Turn to **147**.

"Who do you think attacked Professor Varnum?" Turn to **217**.

39

A sudden cry from somewhere nearby has you hurrying out of the room. You can't be sure, but you thought it sounded like Professor Varnum.

As you emerge onto the landing you see no more than the shadow of a figure leaving the same location.

As you consider giving chase, you see Dr Harrow approaching from the right.

However, your attention is caught by what appears to be a startling rearrangement of the furniture on the landing.

Opposite the top of the stairs is the alcove that you barely registered before, so unremarkable was it. Within it stands a bookcase and a reading chair, set beneath a window that looks out over the grounds of the house to the east.

However, your eye is drawn to it now since the bookcase appears to have been pulled forward so that it is almost entirely blocking the entrance to the reading nook. It is only as you draw closer that you realize the bookcase, in fact, forms a secret door – one that is currently being held open by a body. The faint glow of an electric light comes from the room that lies beyond it.

Drawing closer, you see that it is Otto Varnum who is propping the bookcase-door open. He is lying on his left side with his back to you.

As you crouch down to see if he is still breathing, you hear the commotion of others arriving on the scene.

"What have you done?" Horace Trenholm demands from behind you.

"Nothing," you start to protest, "I heard a cry and when I came to investigate, I found the professor like this!"

"Here, let me take a look at him," Dr Harrow says wearily, moving in next to you.

Turn to **85**.

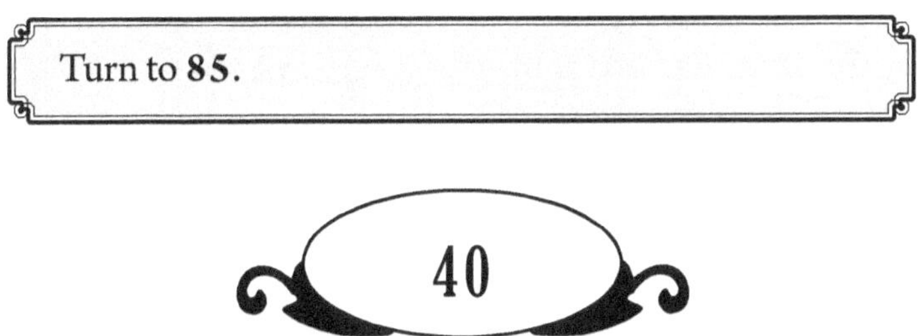

40

Comfort yourself, knowing that you are one of that number with whom I shall share the Mother's gifts.

What is that supposed to mean?

Who is the Mother? And what are her gifts? And who else

is among that number with whom I shall share the Mother's gifts? Could it be the people who have been invited to Harcourt House this evening? Could it include you?

Take +**1 INTELLECT** and the SECRET: *Hidden Three.*

41

The study was where everything in this horrid house began, so you decide to see if something might have been missed previously. But where do you want to search for clues in particular?

42

Unable to move, you feel like a prisoner trapped inside your own body, only able to act as an observer and nothing more, as the spiders haul the struggling attorney ever higher. Take ⁻**1 WILLPOWER**.

"Oh God, no!" Trenholm howls, suddenly regaining his voice and the ability to move. Sprinting the length of the hall, he yanks open the front door of the house and still yelling – "No! No! No!" – disappears into the fogbound night.

Make an initiative test. Roll one die and add your **WILLPOWER**. You may spend **1 RESOURCE** to roll two dice and pick the highest. What's the result?

> Total of 10 or more: turn to **226**.
> 9 or less: turn to **246**.

43

You are keen to learn what kind of man Elijah Harcourt is, and examining what is to be found within his study – his inner sanctum, as it were – seems like a good place to start. Take **+1 INTELLECT**.

While Dr Bellweather searches the area around the desk for the spider that bit the wealthy recluse, you choose where you want to look.

> To peruse the bookshelves that cover the walls, turn to **255**.
> To search the top of Harcourt's desk, turn to **155**.
> To scour the floor of the study, turn to **115**.

44

You eventually fend off the horrors, but not before several of them have wounded you with the stabbing tips of their chitinous claw-tipped limbs.

Take - **2 HEALTH**.

> If your **HEALTH** score is greater than zero, turn to **27**.
> If not, this is ... **The End.**

45

The spiders continue to scurry all over you. You can feel their hairy limbs on every exposed part of your skin, in your ears and your nostrils. You find yourself retreating from the sleepers in their cocoons, so desperate are you to remove yourself from the vicinity of the swarm.

You are going to have to try a different approach, but what will it be?

Attack the Harcourt-spider directly: turn to **245**.

See if you have something you could use against the inhuman horror: turn to **197**.

Use magic: turn to **82**.

Flee from the house: turn to **126**.

Try to escape the attic by passing through the portal into the cave beyond: turn to **18**.

46

"Where were you when Professor Varnum was attacked?" you ask Ward.

The attorney laughs in derision, in response to your question. "I don't think I'll even deign to honor that with an answer."

"Peregrine and I were both here together in the parlor," says the young woman. "We have been ever since my uncle was carried upstairs."

"But that's not entirely accurate, is it?" you point out. "After all, after Dr Bellweather was bitten and fell ill, you went into the hall to wait for medical aid to arrive."

"Yes, and not long after I decided to wait in the parlor instead with Peregrine."

"But he could have snuck upstairs while you were still in the hall," you suggest.

"No, he couldn't," corrects Isabel. "I was sitting in a chair facing the grandfather clock, not the front door, and would have seen him out of the corner of my eye if he had gone upstairs. The only person I saw go upstairs between Cora being taken away and now was you."

"Yes," says the attorney, rounding on you, "where were you when Otto was attacked?"

Take -**1 INTELLECT** and the SECRET: *Fear the Falcon.*

It isn't too long before you are standing outside the Rope and Anchor, the best-known tavern in the Harborside area. It has long been a spot that both the itinerant sailor and the more adventurous tourist can drop anchor, partake of liquor – in flagrant defiance of the Prohibition laws – and catch up on the news of the day.

Entering the establishment, you buy yourself a drink – feeling giddy and decadent for doing so – and settle down at a corner booth, immersing yourself in the general hubbub and tuning in to individual conversations as they come to your attention. Take +**1 RESOURCE**.

As you sit there, unassuming, you hear mention of an academic looking for help in finding the wreck of a pirate ship that sank somewhere off the coast around the decrepit fishing town of Innsmouth, talk of rival gangs clashing in Arkham's Merchant District, and rumors concerning a religious group zealously dedicated to an entity called the Lord of Swarms. But you do not overhear any chatter about Harcourt House or what might be occurring there this evening.

Determined to find out for yourself, you drink up and leave.

Turn to **150**.

48

Exiting Harcourt's bedroom, you suddenly catch sight of something moving on the other side of the landing. You get the ominous feeling that someone just ducked into the shadows of the vestibule that leads to the "Museum."

If you want to follow them and investigate further, turn to **287**.

If not, and you have a [SHIRT BUTTON], turn to **282**.

If not, but you do not have a [SHIRT BUTTON], turn to **202**.

Skittering, crawling, threading their way into your sleeves, your hair, the corners of your mouth, there are spiders all over you. You had thought you could handle this, that it would be unpleasant but tolerable, maybe even over quickly, but it's not as bad as you thought it would be – it's worse!

This isn't a tingle of unease – it's a full-body attempted infestation, a relentless tide of legs and mandibles, and you can't tell if it's one spider crawling across your ribs or a hundred. You flail, but they cling on. They are even inside your collar now. You thought you knew fear, but this is panic wrapped in silk, unremitting and alive.

Take ⁻**1** **SANITY** and gain the Weakness {**ARACHNOPHOBIA**}, if you do not already have it.

Roll one die and divide the result by 2, rounding fractions up. Then deduct this number of **HEALTH** points.

> If your **HEALTH** score is higher than zero, turn to **100**.
>
> If not, then this is… **The End.**

Running your hand over the surface, you don't find any hidden buttons that open a secret compartment. However, as you stroke the blotting pad, you do feel something under your fingertips.

You pause and run your fingers over the absorbent paper

again. You can feel the impressions left by a pen – formed, you suspect, when Harcourt was writing the letters.

Angling the desk lamp, the indentations are brought into shadowed relief, becoming clearer, and you are able to work out what is "written" there.

most delicate – the preservation of Dr Luther Harrow, whose reputation trembled then upon the brink of annihilation. You accomplished the task with admirable dispatch and thus were our accounts balanced.

Take + **1 CLUE**.

> Perhaps keeping track of this half-formed letter might be prudent. Turn to **99**.

51

Exploring the Central Hill area, you are amazed by the number of ornate mansions within Kingsport. But these beautiful houses are not all owned by people who call Kingsport home – some are holiday homes, belonging to many of Arkham's prominent families. Some wealthy elites reside here during the summer – reveling in the seaside entertainments and lavish parties – but others enjoy making Kingsport their home forever. The town is well known for its social gatherings that are the source of gossip and scandal, all documented in the Kingsport Gazette.

However, Kingsport is a place where social standing is often considered of greater worth than anything so base as money or other financial assets. It is also a place that has a preoccupation with the occult, and seances or even sessions of spirit photography often form part of the social gatherings that the great and the good of the town attend.

You walk the wide avenues of the affluent neighborhood with their sweeping views of the town and its bustling harbor, shaded by ancient elms. The area exudes an air of coastal grandeur and genteel isolation. Despite its serene appearance, an eerie stillness clings to the stately New England homes, as if they are sleeping, and your mere presence here might wake them.

Eventually, you finally find the chance encounter you are looking for when a portly middle-aged woman leaves one of the grand houses. Her manner suggests to you that she could easily work at the house, perhaps as a cook, and so you wave and then engage her in conversation, asking if she can direct you to Harcourt House.

"You're in the wrong part of town," she says. "Harcourt House isn't in Kingsport itself. It stands on the top of the cliffs. It's said that from the top floor windows you can see right across the bay to North Point Lighthouse – when the mists aren't in, of course."

"Do you know it well?" you ask.

She shrugs. "Only by reputation."

"And what reputation would that be?"

Glancing up and down the street, she says, "It has a strange atmosphere, is all."

"What sort of atmosphere?" you ask.

"I don't rightly know," she replies, a faraway look in her eyes. "But I've seen the place many times."

"You've been there?"

"No!" she suddenly snaps, her soft musing broken. "I said

I've seen it. In my dreams… In my nightmares… I want to visit it, but I know if I do…"

She shudders and pulls her cloak closer around her, eyeing you suspiciously before drawing back. "I must be on my way. But if I were you, I'd think twice about going there. Good day." And with that she hurries off in the direction of the Harborside. Take + **1 CLUE**.

Time is pressing and so you decide to make your way to Harcourt House – but the cook's warning makes you feel wary of what awaits you.

Turn to **150**.

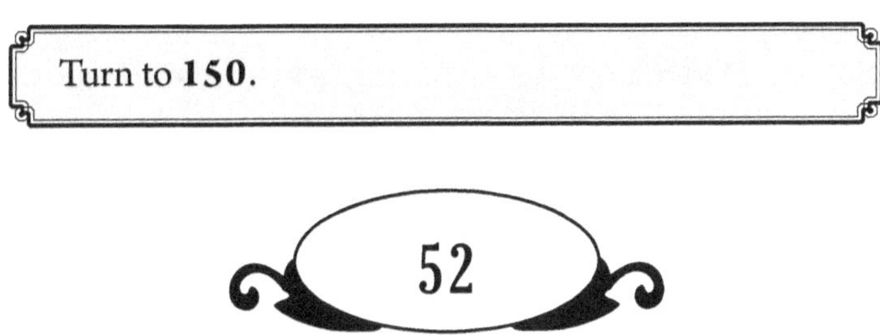

52

The mists of Kingsport seem to have an enigmatic hold over the town and its inhabitants. And now they have power over you as well. But regardless of that fact, you are sure you have made the right choice in putting the walls of the house between you and the insidious vapors.

Take - **1 WILLPOWER** but + **1 SANITY,** and the SECRET: *The Mists of Kingsport.*

If you have a [**SHIRT BUTTON**], turn to **282**.
If not, but you have some [**PINCE-NEZ GLASSES**], turn to **10**.
If you do not have any of the above items, turn to **96**.

53

Horace Trenholm is closest to you. Grabbing him by the shoulders, the gossamer webs sticking to your hands, you shake him violently, calling out his name as you do so.

Isabel does the same to Peregrine Ward, but while his face pulls the most unsettling expressions, he does not wake. When Trenholm doesn't stir either, you turn your attention to Dr Cora Bellweather. And when she won't wake up, you move on to Dr Luther Harrow.

But no matter how hard you try, you cannot wake the sleepers. Realizing that there is nothing you can do for them and fearing that the longer you remain here the less likely it is that you will escape alive, with one final shake of the doctor's shoulders, you make for the stairs.

Roll one die and deduct 1 if you have the {SURVIVOR} Ability.

If the total is equal to or less than your **HEALTH**, turn to **29**.
If the total is greater than your **HEALTH**, turn to **86**.

54

The museum is dominated by numerous display cases, filled with all manner of bizarre objects – some little more than shaped and polished stones, others primitive weapons made of bamboo with obsidian blades, and intricate artifacts skillfully carved from jade, ivory, and alabaster. On one wall is what appears to be a large, framed drawing, while contained within a cabinet that takes the form of a glass-topped table is a series of black and white photographs.

Blinds cover every window, keeping damaging sunlight out during the day, and leaving the room lit by a few desultory wall lamps.

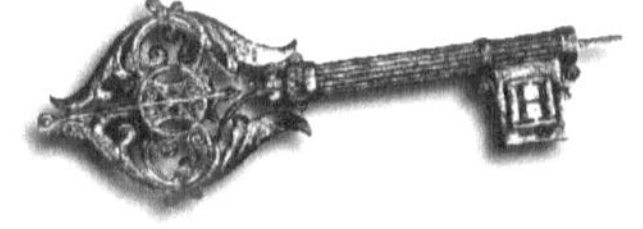

55

The truth behind why you have been summoned to Harcourt House on this particular night is a mystery, but what other secrets are waiting to be uncovered here?

During the struggle, the needle somehow ends up stuck in your side. The initial stab of pain is swiftly followed by a not unpleasant sensation of warmth radiating throughout your body.

"I'm sorry!" Harrow cries. "I didn't mean to… oh my god, it wasn't intended for you. It was for me." He sounds defeated.

The warmth gives way to drowsiness. Your head starts to spin.

"What do you mean?" you ask, slurring your words.

And then his confession pours out of him, but you only pick up parts of it as you battle Morpheus, god of dreams, to stay awake. Take -**1 HEALTH** and -**2 COMBAT**.

"A patient died… In rash despair I confided in him. He dealt with the matter… Peregrine Ward made the problem go away… But from that moment on… Harcourt as good as owned me."

Take +**1 CLUE** and the SECRET: *King of Dreams*.

Turn to **182**.

"You're not going to leave me alone, are you?" Isabel nearly wails.

"Like Ward said, stay here and you'll be fine," you tell her. "Anyway, he said he'd be back in a minute."

So, which room do you want to visit now?

The study: turn to **17**.
The library: turn to **181**.
The museum: turn to **142**.
The recently revealed secret room behind the bookcase: turn to **74**.
Elijah Harcourt's bedroom: turn to **62**.
Alternatively, if you want to leave the house and look outside, turn to **91**.

Moving the chair out of the way, you ease open the secret door. And as you do, you see the mummified corpse standing there, motionless. But only for a moment.

The mummy comes to sudden, unnatural life again – its clothes rippling with the movements of things squirming about beneath – and throws itself at you.

Turn to **141**.

You manage to fend off the mummified corpse as you retreat toward the entrance to the hidden room. Upon reaching the bookcase-door, you dare to give your attacker a shove that sends it stumbling backward. You use the opportunity to throw yourself through the door and slam it shut behind you.

You remain where you are, pressing your body against the bookcase as you recover your wits, half-expecting the mummy to try to force its way out of the room at any moment. But after several minutes and having not felt any pressure against the door or the reverberations of something beating at it from the other side, you dare to step away.

Nothing happens, but you push the alcove's reading chair up against the bookcase, just to be doubly sure.

You assess your injuries but appear to have escaped your encounter with the mummy with no more than a torn sleeve and the promise of the sight of that desiccated face every time you close your eyes for the foreseeable future.

Record the [TORN SLEEVE] on your Character Sheet, take +1 DOOM and the SECRET: *Mummy's Boy*.

If you have a [SHIRT BUTTON], turn to **282**.
If not, but you have some [PINCE-NEZ GLASSES], turn to **10**.
If you do not have either of these items, turn to **96**.

"Oh God, no!" Trenholm howls, suddenly regaining his voice and the ability to move. Sprinting the length of the hall, he yanks open the front door of the house and still yelling – "No! No! No!" – disappears into the fogbound night.

And all the time the spiders continue to haul Peregrine Ward higher and higher toward the ceiling.

> To try to help Ward, turn to **263**.
> To chase after Trenholm, turn to **22**.
> To do nothing, turn to **226**.

"Well, I'm going to the attic," you tell Dr Harrow. You turn to Isabel. "Are you coming with me or are you going to stay with him?"

The young woman's hesitation tells you all you need to know and so you set off alone.

Beyond the vestibule that leads to Elijah Harcourt's museum on the second floor you follow a shadowed passageway to the top of a narrow flight of servants' stairs. This is how Knott and the housemaids go about their business without getting in the way of – or even being seen by – the master of the house and his guests.

You continue to follow the servants' passage and soon arrive at the foot of another narrow staircase. This one can only lead to the attic.

Hearing the creak of floorboards behind you, you start to turn. But then something heavy strikes you between your shoulder blades, and then cracks you over the head, the force of the blow sending you tumbling into oblivion. Take -1 **HEALTH**.

Turn to **283**.

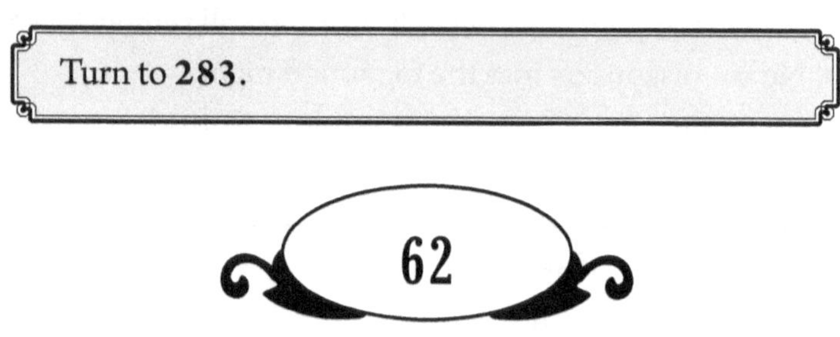

62

You find the door to Elijah Harcourt's bedroom open, the glow of a bedside lamp bathing it in a comforting orange glow.

If you have some [PINCE-NEZ GLASSES], turn to **8**.
If not, but you have a [FOSSIL FANG], turn to **88**.
If you have neither of these things, turn to **148**.

63

"Where do you think it could be?" you ask the arachnologist, joining Dr Bellweather on your knees under the desk.

"Most spiders prefer dark, undisturbed areas, such as the corners of rooms and under furniture."

You twist your head around, fearing that a spider might drop on you from the underside of the desk, but there is nothing there.

"The bite on Harcourt's neck looked nasty," you remark as you turn your attention to scouring the rug on which the desk stands. "Do you have any idea what kind of spider it was?"

"It's very hard to tell from a bite. Different people react in different ways."

"I only thought you might know because you are an expert in the field of arachnology," you persist, standing up.

"Oh, I see. Well, the same answer applies, unfortunately." She blushes. You can almost feel the heat of her burning cheeks there under the desk. "Well, I mean, a bite like that could have been caused by all kinds of venomous species."

"But one that induces what would appear to be a coma in mere moments?" you ask.

"Well, there's Atrax robustus, the funnel-web spider, for one. Its venom causes sweating, drooling, muscle spasms, an elevated heart rate, and difficulty in breathing. It has been known for people bitten by a funnel-web to slip into a coma or suffer respiratory failure and die, but that particular species is native to eastern Australia." She pauses, thoughtful, before continuing.

"Then there's the Brazilian wandering spider, which lives in Central and South America. It is possessed of a potent neurotoxic venom that can cause severe pain, loss of muscle control, and respiratory paralysis as well. In severe, untreated cases, this can progress to coma or death, especially in vulnerable individuals, but never as quickly as this.

"The venom of the redback and various widow spiders is quite horrible indeed. Being bitten by one of those rarely results in the victim going into a coma, although seizures, shock, and unconsciousness can occur."

Take +**1 CLUE**.

"That's incredibly fascinating and equally terrifying," you say.

Dr Bellweather shrugs. "Spiders have simply evolved to survive. It's natural. Our fears, on the other hand, are a bit inflated, all things considered."

You nod, absorbing her words. "Perhaps I shall go and let the others know we've been unsuccessful," you say.

"I'll stay here and keep looking," she says.

Turn to **173**.

64

The horrors easily overcome you, but you are still conscious as they bind you in thick silk, which they extrude from puckered spinnerets at the ends of their abdomens. It is almost a relief when they bind your head in silk, so you don't have to look at the pumping sphincters of the spiders anymore, and before long you are completely immobile.

Trussed up like this, you are hauled up into the branches of a tree and left hanging upside down. Gradually, with blood pooling in your head, you find it harder to breathe. As your lungs are compressed by heavier organs, you lose consciousness. As a result, you remain ignorant of your fate, which is probably for the best.

SECRET: *Spiders and Flies.*

The End.

A friendly introduction describes Kingsport as "a place of great antiquity and charm, where the sea mist veils both past and present alike," emphasizing its "honest fisherfolk," "ancient houses," and "healthy sea air."

Replete with footnotes, *Olde Kingsport and Its Curiosities – A Visitor's Handbook to the Town by the Sea* – contains a brief history of Kingsport from its origins as a Puritan settlement to a prosperous center for whaling and maritime trade including a whole chapter about its harbor, a list of churches and meeting-houses, and more importantly, a list of inns and other drinking-houses.

Flicking through, near the end you come to a chapter entitled "Legends of Olde Kingsport," and the book metamorphoses from a visitor's guide to a repository of supernatural tales. Among them is a story about a phantom sailor who walks the docks at moonrise, another describes the dreamers who wander the mist-shrouded lanes in their sleep, never to be roused, and the Kingsport Choir – a sound like distant chanting that is only heard on Midwinter's Eve.

Take **+1 CLUE**, and if you want to take the book with you, record **[OLDE KINGSPORT AND ITS CURIOSITIES]** on your Character Sheet.

Turn to **110.**

"Don't go out there," Isabel Harcourt says, putting a hand to your arm. "Please."

You peer into the mist, but it forms such an impenetrable wall that you can see nothing else.

"The danger is here, inside the house," you tell her. "Not out there."

"You don't know that," she replies, her tone insistent. She tightens her grip on your arm.

> If you want to give in to her wishes, turn to **156**.
> If you want to show her you can be just as insistent and go out into the mist, turn to **186**.

"I don't know," replies Trenholm. "I don't want to know. But he was obsessed with them. Maybe that's why the people down in Kingsport steer clear of the place. I wish I'd done the same."

"When you say he was obsessed with spiders, do you mean with collecting them?"

"Anything to do with them. I mean, we're standing in his private museum and there's nothing in here that doesn't have something to do with spiders. He and Otto used to collect stories and myths, too, they were bad for each other, egging each other on. That was until they fell out, of course."

"So, they were friends?"

"Couldn't have been better friends, if you know what I mean."

"What did they fall out over?"

"Something about Elijah stealing Otto's research." He looks at you darkly. "But I did hear another rumor."

"And what was that?"

"Something to do with a ritual. It was supposedly in some text Otto found, or translated, or something. Apparently, Elijah wanted to give it a go – put it into practice, as it were – but Otto thought that was going too far."

"Too far? Why?"

"Two words: blood sacrifice."

Take **+1 CLUE** and **+1 DOOM**.

The explorer won't be drawn on the subject further, but maybe you could ask him something else.

To ask what service Trenholm provided for Harcourt, turn to **97**.

To ask what Harcourt wrote in his letter to the explorer, turn to **147**.

To ask him who he thinks could have attacked Professor Varnum, turn to **217**.

If you are done interrogating the explorer, turn to **257**.

68

"Loosen his collar," Harrow instructs you as, with shaking hands, he unbuttons the professor's waistcoat.

As you do as you are bidden, Varnum suddenly takes a gasping breath and his eyelids flicker open.

"It's all right," you tell him as he grabs your arm, his eyes rolling. "You're going to be all right. Dr Harrow's here."

The professor's gaze rests on you, and his lips open as if he is about to speak.

Make a concentration test. Roll one die and add your **INTELLECT** and your **WILLPOWER**. You may spend **1 RESOURCE** to roll two dice and pick the highest. What's the result?

Total of 10 or more: turn to **189**.
9 or less: turn to **169**.

Despite the horror and mind-wrenching impossibility of it all, you manage to keep your wits about you. With the thing that was once Elijah Harcourt in front of you and Knott behind you, and Isabel Harcourt whimpezring at your side, you are going to have to think fast if you are going to get out of here alive.

"I suppose you arranged the whole thing," you hiss.

"It's what I do," replies Knott.

You turn to look at him and see a sickening smile splitting his sallow face.

"Manage the domestic staff and ensure the smooth operation of the house and estate."

"You mean to say the butler did it?" Isabel shrieks.

"Quite so," replies Knott. "The three watchwords I live by are service, management, and discretion."

Take the SECRET: *The Butler Did It.*

Make a deduction test. Roll one die and add your INTELLECT. You may spend **1 CLUE** to roll two dice and pick the highest. If you have the **{DETECTIVE}**, **{POLICE}** or **{QUICK-WITTED}** Ability, add 1. What's the result?

Total of 10 or more: turn to **92**.
9 or less: turn to **124**.

70

You don't like the look of this. You don't like the look of this at all.

You hurry back to the house at double speed, splashing through a puddle on the ground as you do so, and covering your shoes in mud as a result.

Take **-1 SANITY**, and record the **[DIRTY SHOES]** on your Character Sheet if you haven't done so already.

Opening the door, you let yourself back inside.

Turn to **202**.

71

You deliver the coup de grace, plunging the fossilized fang deep into the horror's body. What little that remains of Harcourt the man gives a piercing scream. The abomination's legs buckle beneath it, and it flops onto the floor of the attic. Revolting fluids ooze from the many wounds you have dealt it.

The otherworldly spiders are close to breaching the web now. The portal to their subterranean kingdom shows no sign of collapsing despite Harcourt's apparent destruction. But then it wasn't Harcourt who was responsible for joining the waking world to the Dreamlands, Knott said. It was the sleepers.

If you want to try to wake the silk-bound sleepers, turn to **53**.
If you think it wiser to flee the attic before the giant spiders join you in the restricted roof space, turn to **29**.

72

Considering what happened the last time you dared to step outside Harcourt House, are you sure you want to brave the mists again?

If you do, turn to **32**.
If not, turn to **52**.

As you study the image and the annotations upon it, it soon becomes clear that it is a drawing of one of the Nazca lines – a group of over 700 geoglyphs made in the soil of the Nazca Desert in southern Peru. Some are over 1,000 feet long but the one that is the subject of this drawing is that of a spider, only 154 feet in length.

It is quite incredible. With its fanged cephalothorax, bulbous abdomen, and eight, angled legs, you marvel at the people who were able to make such an accurate depiction of a spider in the desert when, from the ground, they wouldn't have been able to read the image at all.

Turn to **170**.

The hidden hinges of the bookcase-door groan as you ease it open and enter the room beyond, Otto Varnum having long since been moved to one of the guest bedrooms of Harcourt House.

If you have a [TORN SLEEVE], turn to **58**.
If not, but you have a [SILVER HIP FLASK], turn to **16**.
If you have neither of these items, turn to **188**.

Seeing so many spiders swarming across the ceiling – blotting out the light cast by the chandelier and smothering the wretched attorney – threatens to overwhelm your already beleaguered sanity.

Roll one die, and if you have either the Weakness {CURSED} or {HAUNTED}, add 1.

If the total is equal to or less than your **SANITY**, turn to **60**.
If the total is greater than your **SANITY**, turn to **42**.

Trenholm heads straight to the drinks trolley where he pours himself a large scotch. Downing it in one, he immediately pours himself a second.

"You're thirsty this evening," Peregrine Ward remarks as he pours himself a brandy.

"You want to tell the good professor that," the explorer rails.

"I don't think drink is his particular demon."

"Where is he anyway?" Trenholm asks, looking around the room but finding only you and the attorney there keeping him company.

"I thought I saw him heading to the library," Ward replies.

There is a library here in Harcourt House?

If you want to leave the parlor to look for the library, turn to **191**.
If you're feeling a little thirsty yourself and want to help yourself to a drink, turn to **106**.

An uncomfortable silence hangs in the air around you and you feel compelled to say something to break the tension.

"Are you and your uncle close?" you ask her sympathetically.

"Why do you ask that?" she says, suddenly suspicious.

"I mean, er, does he have any children of his own?"

"Oh no, Uncle Elijah isn't that way inclined," she says with a mirthless laugh. "I had thought we were close, once. He's the only family I have left and I … relied on him."

You say nothing this time, instead letting Isabel fill the silence.

"I got into a little trouble, if I'm honest. I've always had a thing for horses – not riding them, you understand – but Uncle Elijah's money was always there to bail me out, until one day it wasn't. If I'm considerate, perhaps he cut me off to help cure me of my addiction, but I don't think his intentions were altogether that altruistic."

"What makes you say that?" you ask.

"Here, see for yourself," she says, offering you the letter her uncle wrote to her.

You cannot help but accept the following and read it from beginning to end.

My Dearest Isabel,

You will no doubt scoff to find a letter addressed to you from me. Perhaps you will cast it aside unread, as you have so often done with my advice, my warnings, and indeed even my affection. But I ask you now, for your own sake as much as mine, to read on.

You have always possessed a certain brilliance – sharp wit, a reckless spirit, and you are uncommonly gifted in matters of persuasion. But brilliance, untethered, becomes its own destruction. I understand the thrill born of taking risks and that a brilliant mind needs stimulation. But Lady Luck and the horses have not been kind to you, Isabel, and yet still you return to them again and again as if they might finally offer absolution. They will not.

Still, despite your weakness, your debts, your misplaced faith in the fickle mercy of the track, I have not given up on you. I never could, because I know what you are. What you are meant to be.

You are not merely my niece. You are the Door. Through you, the future will be ushered in – whether it comes in beauty or in fire depends only on what lies beyond your threshold. This role is not punishment, nor reward. It is necessity. Destiny. You have been chosen not for your virtue, but for your capacity. Even ruin can be a vessel, Isabel.

You must prepare yourself. The hour approaches when you must give all that you are.

Until then, I remain your affectionate

Uncle Elijah

Isabel Harcourt's moment of introspection, coupled with the contents of the letter, have given you some fresh insights into what could be going on here. Take +**2 CLUES**.

Turn to **96**.

78

As the spiders fall off you and onto the floor, they scuttle away, disappearing between the banisters, under pieces of furniture, and running back up the walls to rejoin the rest of the swarm.

However, in fighting them off you do receive several painful bites.

Roll one die and divide the result by 2, rounding fractions up. Then deduct this number of **HEALTH** points.

Turn to **100**.

"Just a lot of unpleasantness, which at the end of the day counts for nothing. Besides, it wasn't anything he hadn't already said to my face."

> If you want to ask the professor if he is looking for anything in particular, turn to **243**.
> If you want to ask Varnum if he has known Elijah Harcourt long, turn to **31**.
> If you are done interrogating the professor, turn to **219**.

Peregrine Ward glowers at you, while Isabel Harcourt stares at you in disbelief, clearly offended.

"Knott?" she gasps. "He's been my uncle's butler for as long as I can remember. I would trust him with my life. With all our lives!"

"Knott has done nothing but try to help since everything started falling apart this evening," the attorney says, stern. "Not only that, but after he arranged for the housemaids to take Dr Bellweather upstairs after she was bitten, he remained down here."

"Actually, I saw Trenholm come downstairs and head to the kitchen," says Isabel. "He returned only a few moments later with Knott in tow."

"But that was after we had already discovered Professor

Varnum had been attacked," you admit, feeling your cheeks color in embarrassment.

"So, it can't have been Knott then," Ward says triumphantly.

Take ‑ **1 INTELLECT** and the SECRET: *Above Suspicion.*

"But that doesn't change the fact that there is a lunatic hiding in plain sight, somewhere in the house!" Isabel's voice trembles.

"It's all right, my dear," the attorney says, steering her to a chair and encouraging her to sit down. "Stay here. I won't be a moment."

And with that, he leaves the parlor.

You can't help thinking that if you are to get to the bottom of what's going on here, and find whoever it was that stabbed Professor Varnum, you would do better to keep exploring Harcourt House. But then again, perhaps Peregrine Ward is right, and it would make more sense to stay here in the parlor with Isabel. As they say, there is safety in numbers.

If you want to explore the house, turn to **57**.

If you want to remain in the parlor, turn to **77**.

81

As you cross the threshold to the room, you notice something smeared into the carpet. Crouching down to take a closer look, you discover that it is the squashed remains of another spider, like the one that bit Elijah Harcourt and Cora Bellweather. You can see elements of the same scarlet markings.

Looking around the room, it does not look like anything

has been disturbed. You deduce that Otto Varnum was entering the room when he was attacked. Perhaps he saw the spider and stamped on it before it could do to him what its fellow did to the others. Subsequently, if the spider had been positioned and used to attack the professor and failed, no doubt the murderer was then compelled to stab the man with the fossilized fang. But who could have conspired to such a thing?

Clearly, Varnum knew of the existence of this room and was entering it for a reason. But what could that reason be?

Take +**1 CLUE** and the SECRET: *Behind the Bookcase.*

> Turn to **188.**

82

On this night, the autumnal equinox, when the veil between worlds is thin, the fragility of reality can be torn down and reshaped by the non-Euclidean geometries of higher planes of existence. In other words, magic!

But whence comes the magic you intend to use to stop Harcourt and the spiders?

> [**FORGOTTEN CULTS OF HYPERBOREA**]: turn to **237.**
> [**THE SOMNAMBULIST'S PATH**]: turn to **254.**
> The {**SORCERY**} Ability: turn to **297.**
> None of these: turn to **109.**

"Luther?" Ward exclaims, clearly shocked but forcing himself to keep his voice down. "A man who has sworn a literal oath to do no harm?"

Isabel puts a hand to her mouth in shock. "Whatever would make you say such a thing?"

"He arrived on the scene when I did," you reply.

"And how did you get there so quickly?" Ward challenges you.

Take +**1 DOOM** and the SECRET: *Under Suspicion.*

Turn to **277**.

The housemaids are something both less than and greater than human and you are forced to give ground to their savage attacks, which leaves your body bruised and bloodied. Take -**1 HEALTH**.

But then Isabel steps forward to assist you, the horrors she has witnessed having revealed a core of steel at her heart, and she refuses to be subdued.

With the young woman now fighting at your side, armed with a broken chair leg she has found somewhere nearby, you rally. Between you, you take the fight back to the inhuman housemaids.

Turn to **238**.

85

"He's been stabbed!" Dr Harrow exclaims as he rolls the portly professor onto his back. You can see where his blood has soaked the front of his shirt and is even starting to stain the tweed of his waistcoat.

"With what?" asks Trenholm, breathless.

As you scour the surrounding area, your eyes alight on what appears to be a curved stone spike, roughly a foot long and with a reddened tip.

"With this," you say as you pick it up.

Dr Harrow stares at the improvised weapon in disbelief. "What is that?"

"I know," says Trenholm. "It used to have a place of pride in Harcourt's private museum."

"So, what is it?" you ask him.

"It's a fossilized fang."

"Belonging to what?"

"You wouldn't believe me if I told you," Trenholm replies.

"Try me," you say.

"A spider."

"Poppycock! You don't get spiders that big!" exclaims Harrow.

Your gaze moves from the alleged fossil in your hand to Professor Varnum. Record the [FOSSIL FANG] on your Character Sheet and gain +1 RESOURCE.

"Is he alive?" you ask.

"Yes," replies the doctor, "but I don't know for how long. I need to get a better look at the stab wound. Will you help me move him?"

You and Harrow drag the professor's body, as carefully as you can, away from the open door.

"Where's the medical assistance I was promised?" he snaps. "Somebody get Knott!"

"I'm on it," says Trenholm, racing back down to the hall below, taking the stairs two at a time.

But what are you going to do?

If you want to volunteer to help Harrow tend to Varnum, turn to **68**.

If you want to find out what lies behind the bookcase-door, turn to **116**.

If you want to investigate Harcourt's private museum, turn to **142**.

If you want to go downstairs to tell the others what's happened, turn to **233**.

While you have been otherwise preoccupied, the spiders from the cave have reached the web-portal and two of them squeeze through it between the strands. Their abdomens are bulbous, the color of pallid flesh, while their legs are like giant articulated, black thorns.

The horrors leap on you and Isabel before you can escape. They subdue you with their venom, introduced into your bloodstream via a painful bite, before tearing you apart with their razor legs.

You might have stopped Knott from sacrificing you so that his master could achieve his apotheosis, but the house of spiders has claimed two more victims this night, nonetheless.

Take the SECRET: *The Spiders of Leng.*

Final score: 0 stars.

The End.

Not bothering to return to the drive, you hurry toward the house across the lawn, not daring to look back either. Even when you are safe inside the manor once more, you cannot get the image of the spider emerging from Trenholm's mouth out of your head.

Make a note on your Character Sheet that you have [DIRTY SHOES] if you haven't done so already, and gain the Weakness {HAUNTED} if you do not already have it.

Turn to **202.**

Entering the room, the first thing you notice is the bulging mass under the covers of the four-poster bed. It takes you a moment to realize that it is Elijah Harcourt. His body has become grotesquely swollen.

You approach the bed warily, peeking around so you can see Harcourt's face. It is bright purple and horribly puffy, as if he is suffering a severe allergic reaction. His lips look like two fat black slugs, while his cheeks appear to be permanently puffed out. His eyes are swollen shut, but you're certain that he remains unconscious. His breathing is a labored rasp, but at least he is still breathing.

Lying on the bedside table by the lamp is a discarded medicine vial, which you assume was left here by Dr Harrow. You must have just missed him. The vial is empty.

Seeing what is happening to Elijah Harcourt disturbs you deeply. Take -**1 SANITY** and +**1 DOOM**.

You can't believe one of the servants isn't sitting with him in his room, considering his significantly worsening condition. That said, there's nothing you can do for him, so you have a simple choice to make.

> If you want to search the room for clues, turn to **28**.
> If you want to leave the room immediately, possibly to find help for Elijah Harcourt, turn to **7**.

"You think Varnum stabbed himself?" Ward exclaims. "While I'll admit that it is physically possible, why would he do it?"

"He has been agitated this evening," Isabel points out.

"But he wasn't suicidal!" snaps Ward. "Haven't we all been under a lot of stress recently?"

"But he has been possessed of such a dreadful melancholy since he and Uncle Elijah had their falling out," Isabel persists. "What was that about, anyway?"

"I don't know," the attorney replies hastily.

"But if he didn't harm himself," Isabel goes on, her face falling, "then we have to face the fact that someone else in this house did."

"It's going to be all right, my dear," the attorney says, steering her to a chair and encouraging her to sit down. "Stay here. I won't be a moment."

And with that, he leaves the parlor.

You can't help thinking that if you are to get to the bottom of what's going on here, and find whoever it was that stabbed Professor Varnum, you would do better to keep exploring Harcourt House. But then again, perhaps Peregrine Ward is right, and it would make more sense to stay here in the parlor with Isabel. As they say, there is safety in numbers.

> If you want to explore the house, turn to **57**.
> If you want to remain in the parlor, turn to **77**.

The Somnambulist's Path is a slender volume bound in pale leather. The prose within is fragmented, alternating between cryptic instructions, descriptions of dream-visions, and philosophical musings. Its unnamed author also claims certain passages are sourced from older dream-manuscripts.

The book asserts that sleepwalking is not a malady but, in fact, the soul striving to reach the Dreamlands. But this is merely the first step on the path. It describes breathing exercises, symbolic gestures and stranger things – whispered invocations – that supposedly weaken the tether between the body and the dreaming soul. Some passages even suggest using narcotics such as laudanum to achieve the state required to take the next step on the path. The author paints the Dreamlands not as a fantastical realm but an inversion of waking reality – more mutable and more treacherous, but also a source of secret knowledge.

Take +**1** **CLUE**, and if you want to take the book with you, record [**THE SOMNAMBULIST'S PATH**] on your Character Sheet.

Turn to **110**.

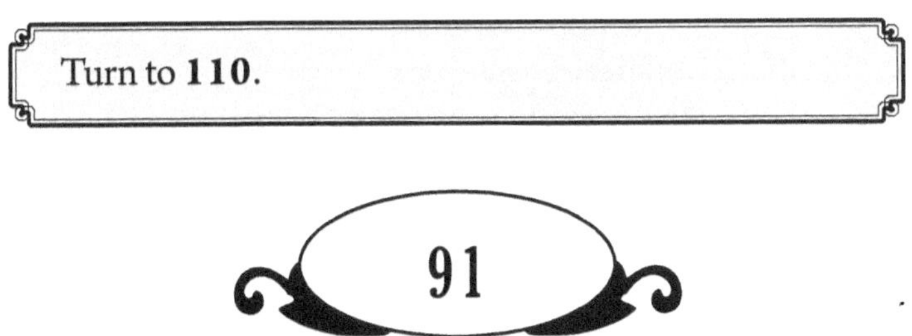

Opening the front door, you see that a thick mist surrounds the house. Kingsport's notorious climate has struck again. In fact, the fog is so thick that you can barely see the gravel drive

at the bottom of the steps. And you cannot see the avenue of
red maple trees that line the drive at all.

If you have [DIRTY SHOES], turn to 72.
If not, turn to 32.

92

"You mean to say you were acting on the orders of another,"
you say.

"I have been in Mr Harcourt's service for thirty-three years,"
replies Knott. "I live only to serve."

Thirty-three years? That's longer than many marriages.

"So, why would you want to hurt him?" asks Isabel,
clearly struggling to hold it together and stop her mind from
unravelling in the face of such unrelenting horror.

"This was Harcourt's plan all along," you tell her, the pieces
all coming together. "That's why he invited everyone here, on
this particular night."

"The autumnal equinox," says Knott. "The threshold
between light and dark, a time of transition that marks the
thinning of the veil between worlds."

The thinning of the veil between worlds. The butler's words
echo inside your head as you look beyond the great web to the
impossible cave. You think you are beginning to understand
what is happening here.

Take +1 INTELLECT, +1 CLUE, and the SECRET:
The Butler Didn't Do It.

Turn to 124.

93

You do not know why you were summoned to Harcourt House, but you do not intend to find out either. Crossing the hall to the front door, you turn the handle and open the door, only to have it slammed shut again as the butler Knott suddenly places himself between you and your means of egress.

"Where do you think you are going?" he growls.

"I'm leaving," you state emphatically, pulling on the handle once more.

"Mr Harcourt invited you here for a reason," the butler says, his voice as cold as the look in his eyes. "Do you not want to learn why?"

Knott's words pluck at your naturally curious spirit. There is certainly a mystery to be solved here. But you do not like the way Knott is acting.

You let your hand drop from the handle.

"Now, can I suggest you help yourself to a drink in the parlor while we await the result of Dr Harrow's examination of Mr Harcourt?" Knott suggests as he demurely looks at the ground, seeming to remember his place and that you are a guest.

Take +**1 CLUE** but -**1 WILLPOWER**.

Turn to **173**.

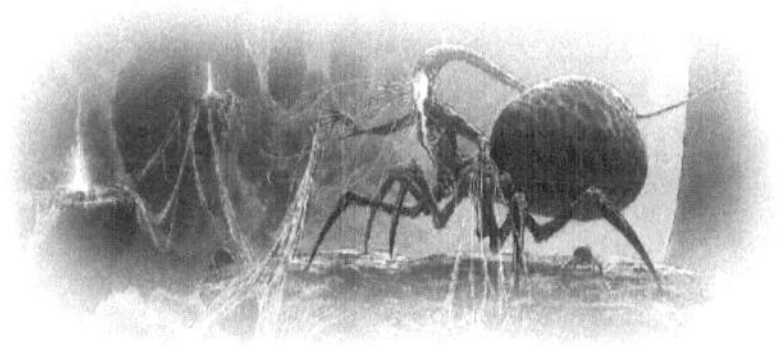

As you make your way around the landing, past an alcove in which stands a bookcase and a reading chair under an east-facing window, your eye is drawn to the ornate chandelier that is suspended from the ceiling.

The bulbs in their settings emit a low light, but the shadow they cast of the chandelier itself on the cracked plaster above reminds you far too much of a monstrous spider clinging to the ceiling. Take -**1 SANITY.**

Turn to **62.**

The pattern puts you in mind of overlapping spiderwebs, only each one is a maze, and you are almost afraid to wonder where you would end up if you followed one of those strange mazes to its center. Take -**1 SANITY.**

Transfixed by the images conjured by the warp and weft of the carpet, you almost miss the [EMPTY GLASS JAR] that is lying there, not far from the desk. You pick it up and find that it is empty; its lid is also nearby.

Could someone have released the spider in here on purpose? Take +**1 DOOM.**

If you want to keep the [EMPTY GLASS JAR], record it on your Character Sheet.

Turn to **289.**

Hearing an unexpected cry, you leap into action. Following the sound, you hurry to the central staircase of the house. What you see there fills you with horrified disbelief. Peregrine Ward appears to be suspended from the chandelier that hangs from the apex of the ceiling.

He is hanging by a multitude of sticky strands being spooled by the swarm of spiders that covers the chandelier, the chain supporting the light, as well as the cracked plaster of the ceiling. You have never seen anything like it. The spiders surge and cover everything, and all you can see now is a writhing wave of bristly black bodies that moves like an undulating carpet.

Isabel Harcourt, Horace Trenholm and Dr Harrow now also appear, observing the horrifying spectacle, sobbing, moaning in revulsion, and staring open-mouthed in silent shock respectively.

As you watch, your body petrified, the frightfulness of what you are witnessing robs you of the ability to move. The spiders start to descend their web strands and run all over Ward's body until soon you can see little of the man beneath the black-furred mass, although you can still hear his increasingly desperate screams. Take -**1 SANITY**.

Something suddenly falls from amidst the mass of spiders and lands at your feet on the floor. They are Peregrine Ward's glasses. Record the **[PINCE-NEZ GLASSES]** on your Character Sheet.

> If you have the Weakness
> **{ARACHNOPHOBIA}** or **{FEAR OF
> INSECTS}**, turn to **75**.
> If not, turn to **60**.

"I got him a lot of this stuff," Trenholm says, taking in the glass cabinets with a wave of his hand.

There are artifacts from all over the world here – from Brazil to Burma, by way of West Africa and Greece, and everywhere in between. There is even a Huichol yarn painting from Mexico alongside a pre-Raphaelite painting of Morgan le Fay, the reviled sorceress from Arthurian myth, with her cloak painted to look like it is made from silken cobwebs.

It seems that every major culture in the world has venerated spiders in one form or another for millennia.

"I wasn't sorry to see the back of that one," he says, indicating a storytelling staff from Haiti depicting Anansi the spider. He takes a swig from the battered hip flask.

"It must have cost a lot to fund all those expeditions," you say.

"It did. He still owes me for the last one."

"Which one was that?" you ask.

"Oh no, it's not on display. It's in here." He pats the satchel slung over his shoulder. "But he's not getting it until he pays up. Although, admittedly, I'm not sure when that's going to happen now. I should probably have another word with Peregrine, not that I trust him as far as I could throw him." Take +**1 CLUE**.

To ask what Harcourt put in Trenholm's letter, turn to **147**.

To ask him who he thinks could have attacked Professor Varnum, turn to **217**.

If you are done asking Trenholm questions, turn to **257**.

Forcing your way into the room and kneeling beside Dr Bellweather, you wipe the sweat from the woman's brow, gently telling her that it's all right, that you're there, and she's not alone.

She stirs, her mouth parts, and an unintelligible mumble escapes her lips.

"I'm sorry, what did you say?" you ask softly.

The zoologist's face creases in pain, and she lets out a sigh of frustration. Then she takes another breath and tries again. Only you're still not sure what she said.

It sounded a bit like, "Otto had seen such signs in horrors." But then again it could have been, "We ought to have seen such sins in Horace." Or was it just, "We ought to have seen such signs in horrors"?

Whatever the truth, what could she have meant?

Suddenly someone cries, "Watch out!" and everyone scatters.

Turning, you see a dark shape scuttling toward you on eight legs. You barely have time to react before Horace Trenholm flies into the study, with what appears to be a glass jar in one hand.

He practically throws himself at your feet. The glass crashes against the floor. A moment later, he gets up again. The glass jar is still in his hand, but now with its lid screwed down tight and a hideous arachnid trapped inside it. The spider must be four inches across at least.

Its bulbous black body is covered with strange, skull-like scarlet Rorschach inkblot markings, while its eyes are myriad gleaming black pearls. And then there are the overlarge mandibles, a droplet of clear liquid collecting at the tip of each needle-like fang.

Turn to **244.**

99

Tucked under one corner of the blotting pad you find a torn scrap of paper. On it, once again written in Elijah Harcourt's hand, is a list of seven names, and everyone on it is present this evening, including you! You don't know what it is doing there or what its significance is, but you decide to hang onto it, just in case.

Take + **1 CLUE** and record the [**LIST OF NAMES**] on your Character Sheet.

Turn to **289**.

100

While you have been battling to rid yourself of the spiders, the rest of the swarm has managed to drag Ward up to the ceiling. You watch, helpless, as the attorney – now silent and limp –

becomes subsumed by the seething mass of black-furred bodies. The swarm then starts to move toward what you can see in the suffused light is a hole, the bare lathes of the ceiling's construction visible beneath the broken plaster.

The spiders disappear into this hole, taking Ward with them, until not a single one of the eight-legged horrors remains anywhere within the stairwell.

Take +**2 DOOM** and the SECRET: *Eight-Legged Freaks.*

Turn to **118.**

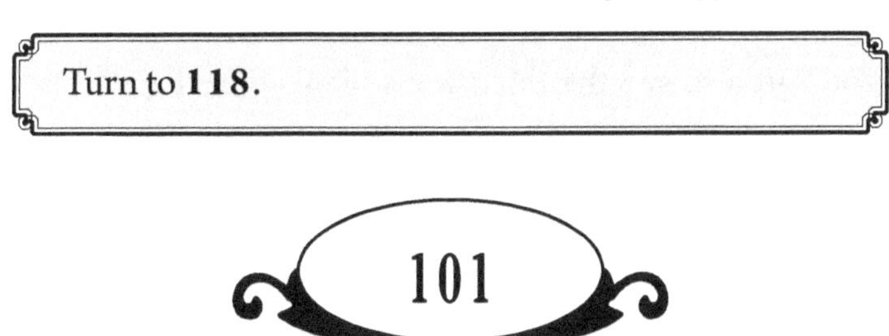

101

Holding the artifact out before you, you see the horrors physically recoil. A susurrus of angry hisses ripples around you as the monsters start to retreat with skittering steps.

Not waiting to see if they recover their courage and start to advance again, you run back toward the house. However, your close encounter with the overgrown spider-monsters leaves you feeling shaken to the very core of your being. Not only that, but your sojourn into the grounds has left you with filthy footwear. Take -1 **SANITY** and record your **[DIRTY SHOES]** on your Character Sheet if you haven't done so already.

You finally make it back to the steps up to the front door, the creatures having returned to their webs among the red maples. Opening the door, you let yourself back inside.

Turn to **282.**

You set off down the drive, away from the house.

Is it your imagination, or is the ever-present mist starting to relinquish its hold on the land and is in retreat? Or perhaps it is because the moon has risen now. But whatever the truth, you can see the red maples more clearly now.

You can also see the thick webs blanketing them. It is as if thousands of spiders have been busy spinning their sticky snares and setting their traps to catch moths and other unwary insects.

Through those webs, backlit by suffused moonlight, you can see a shadowy shape. You feel your throat constrict in fear at the sight of it.

> If you want to approach the web-covered tree, turn to **229**.
> If you would rather head back to the house, turn to **70**.

You are determined to finish what you have started, but you will have to do so quickly, before any reinforcements can arrive.

You may spend **1 RESOURCE** at the start of each round to add 2 to your total for that round.

Round one: roll two dice and add your **COMBAT**. If you

have the {FIGHTER} or {RESOLVED} Ability, add 1.
If you have the Weakness {ARACHNOPHOBIA} or
{CAUTIOUS}, deduct 1. If the total is 10 or more, you win
the first round.

Round two: roll two dice and add your **COMBAT**. If
you have the {TOUGH} Ability, add 1. If you won the first
round, add 1. If you have the {ARACHNOPHOBIA}
Weakness, deduct 1. If your total is 11 or more, you win the
second round.

Round three: roll two dice and add your **COMBAT**.
If you have the {SURVIVOR} Ability, add 1. If you
won the second round, add 2. If you have the Weakness
{ARACHNOPHOBIA}, deduct 1. If your total is 12 or
more, you win the third round.

> If you won two or more rounds, turn to **71**.
> If you lost two or more rounds, turn to **86**.

104

"Where were you when the professor was attacked?" you ask
the young woman.

She stares back at you, her mouth open in an expression
of disbelief. But before she can find the words to express her
annoyance, Peregrine Ward speaks up in her defense.

"She was here in the parlor with me."

"That's right," Isabel says, on the verge of tears.

You look from one to the other. "So you are each other's
alibi."

"Yes," Ward growls. "And who's yours? Where were you when Otto was stabbed?"

Take -**1 INTELLECT** and the SECRET: *Prime Suspect*.

> **Turn to 277**

105

"What about Trenholm?" you say, keeping your voice low.

"Horace?" exclaims Isabel.

The attorney quickly hushes her. "What makes you say that?" he asks.

"He arrived on the scene very soon after Dr Harrow and I did," you explain.

"And where did the doctor appear from?"

"He had been tending to Mr Harcourt, I assume."

"So, what's to say it wasn't Dr Harrow?" asked Ward. "Or you?"

"Did either of you see Trenholm after Cora was bitten?" you ask.

"Yes," says the attorney, "he came in here with me and poured himself a large scotch. Not long after, Isabel joined us from the hall."

"That's right," agrees Isabel, "but then he left. Do you remember?"

"So he did."

"Do you know where he went?" you ask.

The look they exchange tells you all you need to know.

"So, it could have been Trenholm!"

Isabel gives a cry of alarm and collapses into a chair with her head in her hands.

"It will be all right, my dear," the attorney says, patting her on the shoulder. "Stay here. I won't be a moment."

And with that, he leaves the parlor.

You can't help thinking that if you are to get to the bottom of what's going on here, and find whoever it was that stabbed Professor Varnum, you would do better to keep exploring Harcourt House. But then again, perhaps Peregrine Ward is right, and it would make more sense to stay here in the parlor with Isabel. As they say, there is safety in numbers.

> If you want to explore the house, turn to **57**.
>
> If you want to remain in the parlor, turn to **77**.

106

Peregrine Ward fills a glass for you. Taking it, you knock back the brandy, feeling the burn down to your stomach. Take **+1 RESOURCE,** but if this is not the first alcoholic beverage you have partaken of this evening, also take **-1 COMBAT.**

It is then that you notice the envelope addressed to Dr Cora Bellweather, lying where Knott clearly left it in the commotion when everyone rushed back to the study to find her having been bitten by the spider – the same dead spider that is even now inside the [FULL SPECIMEN JAR] in your pocket.

Trenholm has noticed it, too. "We should open it and read it," he says.

"No," says Ward firmly. "It is intended for Dr Bellweather. It is private. It should be left unopened until she is in a fit state to open and read it herself."

"If she comes out of her coma, you mean."

"Precisely."

"Which may never happen."

If you want to snatch up the letter and open it while the two men are arguing, turn to **136**.

If you think that Peregrine Ward is right and that the letter should be left unopened, turn to **166**.

107

Knott suddenly reappears at the entrance to the parlor and beckons you over. Leaving Isabel watching Dr Harrow, you cross the room to where the butler stands in the hallway.

"Is help on the way?" you ask as you approach.

"I have most grave news," he says in hushed tones.

"Then spit it out, man!"

"I just tried to call them again but ..." He breaks off, a pained expression on his face.

"What is it?" you press.

"What's going on? What's the matter?" Isabel asks, suddenly at your side. "Is it my uncle?"

"Knott was just about to tell me something of importance," you tell her. And then, addressing the butler, "So? What has you tongue-tied?"

"Someone has pulled the telephone cord out of the wall," the butler says, casting his eyes at the floor, as if embarrassed.

The sound of a sash being raised has you turning to see Dr Harrow standing at an open window, while the temperature in the parlor drops dramatically.

"Doctor, what are you doing?" exclaims Isabel.

"I'm burning up," Harrow says without turning around. "I need some air."

For a moment, the physician basks before the open window and lets out a loud relieved sigh. And then, in the blink of an eye, he is gone.

It is only as you stand there, stunned motionless, staring at the mist curling outside the window, that you feel absolute terror rush through you. Because something long and gray – several somethings actually – had closed around the doctor's torso and folded him out the window.

A strangled scream dies in Isabel's throat, rousing you to sudden action. You rush across the room and slam the window shut. As you do so, you notice the button lying on the floor and pick it up – it must have come loose from Harrow's shirt. Record the [SHIRT BUTTON] on your Character Sheet and take +2 DOOM.

"Did you see that?" Isabel gasps in a strained whisper. "Did you see what took him? We must help him!"

"There is something I must show you first," the butler says, only a slight warble in his voice. "And I need to show you. I can't just tell you. Quick, come with me."

> If you agree to go with Knott, turn to **269**.
> If not, turn to **235**.

As the maid scampers away, out of the corner of your eye it seems to you that, rather than trotting along the landing, she is scuttling across the wall, her hands and feet spread out at an angle from her body, giving her the disturbing aspect of a huge, clothed spider.

You snap your head around in shock only to see the young woman trotting along the landing once more, on just two legs and no longer clinging to the wall.

Take - **1 SANITY** and the SECRET: *Spider Woman.*

Turn to **96**.

You hear a sound like a walking cane repeatedly tapping against the floorboards as the Harcourt-spider stalks toward you across the attic. Take + **2 DOOM**.

If you want to turn and run from it, turn to **126**.
If you want to stand and fight, turn to **135**.

You suddenly become aware of an unsettling noise. It is coming from the north side of the room and sounds like something is scratching at the window there, as if trying to get in.

If you want to investigate, turn to **121**.
If not, turn to **145**.

Cora Bellweather screams, which startles you more than the scene that greets your eyes within the study.

The room is dimly lit, the lone source of illumination a wrought-iron lamp on a vast, claw-footed mahogany desk that dominates the center of the space. No fire has been laid within the fireplace.

Slumped across the desk is a man dressed in a burgundy smoking jacket. His hair is graying at the temples, and his body appears unnaturally slumped. Take **+1 DOOM**.

"Uncle!" Isabel Harcourt cries out, rushing forward only to be held back by the attorney.

"Elijah?" Professor Otto Varnum whispers in shock.

"Keep back, everyone," orders Dr Harrow, keeping everyone at arm's length as he approaches the body.

You are barely aware of the bookshelves lining the walls of the study, or the eclectic range of objects arrayed upon them. But as the doctor feels for a pulse in the man's neck, you cannot help but notice the letters arranged in a neat fan on the blotting pad in the middle of the desk, bathed in the light of the wrought-iron lamp. There are seven in total.

"He's alive," Dr Harrow announces, and you feel the tension in the air ease.

"What is it?" Professor Varnum asks. "Heart attack? Stroke?"

"It's impossible to say until I've had a chance to examine him properly," Harrow replies. "We need to move him from here and lay him down somewhere. Knott?"

The butler obediently scurries forward. "Yes, Dr Harrow?"

"Help me move him, would you?"

"Yes, doctor, of course."

"I'll help," offers Trenholm.

Harrow carefully leans the comatose Elijah Harcourt back in his seat and then rolls the chair away from the desk on its casters. As Knott and Trenholm go to lift the unconscious man by the ankles and under the arms, Dr Harrow suddenly says, "Hang on a minute, what's this?"

You can all see what the physician has seen now. On the man's neck, under his chin, the flesh is red and swollen.

"Looks like it could be a bite," Harrow says, peering closer. "There's a definite bull's-eye lesion."

"What does that mean?" Isabel asks.

"The wound is almost purple at the center, then there's a white ring around that, and lastly, surrounding all of it is an angry red ring."

"A spider bite?" Dr Bellweather suggests from the entrance to the study.

"Yes," muses the doctor, "it could be. It could very well be."

"Could that explain his current state?" Ward asks.

"Oh, absolutely," says the zoologist before Harrow can respond with a medical diagnosis. "If it was a spider bite, then the spider's venom could have put him into a coma, but that would suggest the culprit is not a spider native to New England."

"Then it is imperative we get him to a hospital as quickly as possible," Dr Harrow says. "There is little more I can do for him here with what I have in my medical bag."

"I shall telephone for assistance immediately," the butler says, leaving the study in a hurry.

"We still need to make Elijah comfortable somewhere," says Harrow.

"His bedroom?" offers Isabel.

"Yes, of course."

"What about the spider?" asks Dr Bellweather, entering the study, crouching down, and peering under the desk. You feel the hairs on the back of your neck rise. "Whatever bit him must still be in this room."

"Then I'm not going in there," says Varnum, remaining just outside of the study.

What do you want to do?

Help Harrow and Trenholm carry Elijah to his bedroom: turn to **23**.

Join Professor Varnum out of the study: turn to **123**.

Join Dr Bellweather in looking for the spider: turn to **63**.

Make the most of the opportunity to look around the study: turn to **43**.

Take a closer look at the pile of letters on the desk: turn to **143**.

Alternatively, if you do not want to spend another second in Harcourt House and would rather leave, turn to **93**.

"Just a lot of unpleasantness, which at the end of the day counts for nothing. Besides, it wasn't anything he hadn't already said to my face."

Turn to **129**.

113

The transformed Harcourt scuttles back to the center of its web, on its strange melding of spider and human limbs, bowed but not beaten. This could be your chance to finish it, or equally it could be an opportunity to make your escape.

Through the portal framed by the silken ropes, you can see

the shadowy spider shapes moving across the cave toward the web. Whatever they are, they appear to have become aware of your presence and are rallying to the aid of their queen's chosen one.

If you want to keep battling the transformed Harcourt, turn to **103**.

If you want to see if you have something you could use to finish it off more quickly, turn to **197**.

If you want to try using magic against the horror, turn to **82**.

If you want to wake the sleepers, turn to **132**.

If you want to use this opportunity to flee the house, turn to **176**.

If you want to escape the attic by climbing through the web into the otherworldly cave beyond, turn to **18**.

114

To your left, beyond a small vestibule, is a polished walnut door bearing the sign "Museum." Directly in front of you is the reading nook, with the door concealed behind the bookcase that leads to the hidden room.

If you want to enter the museum, turn to **142**.
If you want to enter the hidden room, turn to **74**.
If neither of those options appeals, turn to **94**.

The floor of the study is polished black oak, covered with a Turkish rug which is, in turn, covered with an intricate pattern that makes your eyes ache and sting just to look at it. Take **+1 DOOM**.

> If you have a [FULL SPECIMEN JAR], turn to **163**.
> If not, turn to **95**.

Stepping carefully around the professor, you enter the room that lies beyond the bookcase-disguised door. It is lit by a naked lightbulb that bathes the space inside in a dirty yellow illumination.

Make an observation test. Roll one die and add your **INTELLECT**. You may spend **1 CLUE** to roll two dice and pick the highest. If you have the {SEEKER} or {DETECTIVE} Ability, add 1. What's the result?

> Total of 8 or more: turn to **81**.
> 7 or less: turn to **188**.

Trenholm,

Your insolence astonishes me. That you presume to withhold from me what is rightfully mine is nothing short of an outrage. Do not think for one moment that your shabby little act of defiance ennobles you in any way – it makes you nothing more than a toad puffing its throat in the shadow of the serpent.

You complain of accounts unsettled when I have funded your many sojourns to South America from my own pocket. But what are such trifles when set against the great work? Money and ledgers are the currency of ignorant fools. I deal in destiny. And that includes yours.

Let me make this plain – it is you who is in debt to me and, when the reckoning comes, you will settle your account in full. You have mistaken my past unquestioning generosity for weakness, and my civility for indulgence. But no more. The idol you hold will be mine and by keeping it from me, you stand not as its guardian but as a thief – and thieves, as you well know, do not die gently.

Harcourt

Now turn back to the section you just came from.

"They took him!" Isabel finally manages between great shuddering sobs, tears of terror streaming down her face, her whole body shaking, clearly in a state of shock. "They just took him! We must get out of here. Do what Horace did and run and never look back!"

"No," says Dr Harrow, evidently trying hard to remain calm, although his hands are possessed of a palsy all their own. "We have to stick together." He gives you and Isabel a pleading look. Then an idea strikes him. "We should call for help."

"But Knott already did that," she rails at him. "Luther, you're not thinking straight."

"Yes, that's what we should do," he repeats as if he hasn't heard her. "Call for help."

There is another option. You could try to find out where the spiders have taken Ward.

If you want to go along with Dr Harrow's plan, turn to **152**.
If you want to suggest looking for Ward, turn to **134**.
If you want to do something else, turn to **175**.

You're not entirely sure what an empty desk can tell you, but you study its surface closely, nonetheless.

Make an investigation test. Roll one die and add your **INTELLECT**. You may spend **1 CLUE** to roll two dice and pick the highest. If you have the {**DETECTIVE**} or {**SEEKER**} Ability, add 1. What's the result?

> Total of 8 or more: turn to **50.**
> 7 or less: turn to **99.**

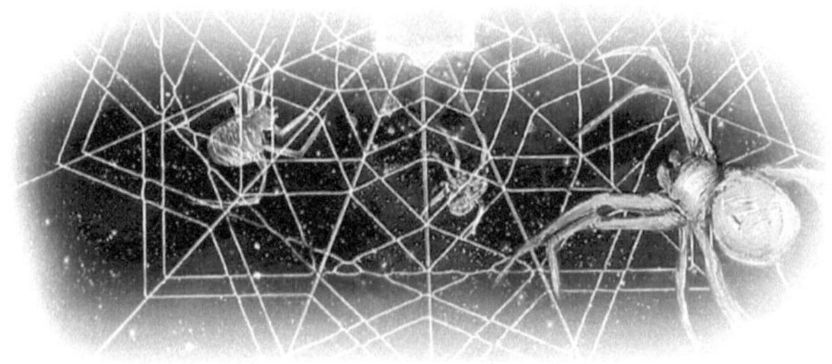

120

As you approach the corner of the room, you can see that Isabel Harcourt is in a state of high dudgeon while Peregrine Ward has his back to you.

The young woman's attention is fixed firmly on the attorney. As you draw closer you hear her say, "I can't believe he cut me off! I mean, what have I really done to deserve that? You must speak to him again for me!"

When she becomes aware of your presence, she quiets immediately. Seeing the shift in attention by the flick of her eyes, Ward turns and takes a step away from Isabel.

Take **+1 CLUE** and the SECRET: *Cut Off.*

"Is there something I can do for you?" the attorney asks.

You offer Ward a polite smile and step forward. "Actually, yes, if you don't mind," you say, your tone conversational. "I've always found the law fascinating, though I admit I know very little about it. You must deal with all kinds of situations. I imagine discretion and precision are your constant companions," you add, your eyes following Isabel Harcourt as she makes her way to the drinks trolley.

The attorney regards you for a moment, then gives a curt nod. "That's one way to put it," he replies, launching into a brief but illuminating overview of his work – drafting trusts, managing estates, navigating inheritance disputes.

As he speaks, you ask thoughtful questions, prompting him to elaborate on key legal principles, the importance of precedent, and the subtle art of negotiation. By the time the conversation winds down, you've gleaned enough to understand not just the mechanics, but the mindset behind legal maneuvering.

Take the Ability {LEGAL KNOWLEDGE}.

You have just one more question you want to ask.

Turn to **280**.

121

Crossing to the window, you draw back the curtains and immediately jump back in shock. For outside, the glass panes are covered with several large spiders – each as big as a tarantula, if not bigger, and covered with gray fur. The spiders are tapping on the glass with their bristling legs, as if testing the strength of the window or looking for a way in.

Beyond this fearful sight, you can see an ash tree that has grown close to the house, and from a hole in the trunk emerge more of the arachnid horrors!

You fling the curtains shut immediately and flee from the library in fear.

Take -**1 WILLPOWER** and the SECRET: *The Ash Tree.*

> If you have a [SHIRT BUTTON], turn to **282**.
> If not, but you have some [PINCE-NEZ GLASSES], turn to **10**.
> If not, but you have a [FOSSIL FANG], turn to **96**.
> If you do not have any of the above items, turn to **162**.

122

The desperate attorney flings you out of the way and, losing your balance, you fall to the floor, hitting your shoulder on the edge of the desk.

Take -**1 HEALTH** and -**1 COMBAT**.

Ward dashes out of the room, slamming the door behind him to slow you down. The papers he burned in the hearth are now no more than curling, flame-licked pieces of black ash.

> If you want to pursue Peregrine Ward, turn to **96**.
> If you would rather search the study to see if there is anything here that might give you a clue as to why he was in here in the first place, turn to **41**.

Professor Varnum returns to the parlor and the drinks trolley, where he tops up his glass again and then promptly downs its contents in one gulp, swallowing audibly.

Peregrine Ward joins him. "So, Otto," he says, "had you and Elijah let bygones be bygones, yet? Because, if you haven't, it doesn't look like you're going to get the chance now."

In response, Otto merely scowls at the attorney and then pours himself yet another drink.

"Peregrine," says Isabel, joining the three of you in the parlor, a bundle of letters in her hand, "we should distribute these."

"My advice is that right now we don't need to do anything," replies the attorney.

"But Uncle Elijah was clearly planning on giving them out. There's one addressed to each of us. That's why we're all here, don't you think?"

"I know why I'm here," Horace Trenholm says as he returns from helping to move Harcourt upstairs.

"And why's that?" asks Professor Varnum.

"The same reason any of us is here," he sneers. "Because we all had a bone to pick with Elijah Harcourt. And when he summoned us here, we knew it might be our only chance to have it out with him."

It may be that the explorer has quite the past with Elijah Harcourt, and clearly the others present do as well, but you had never even heard of the man until he wrote to you, asking you to attend this evening's soiree. Take **+1 CLUE**.

"Where's Dr Harrow?" Ward asks.

"Upstairs with his patient," Trenholm replies. "Giving him a proper examination. He'll join us shortly."

"And what's happened to Knott?"

"Medical assistance is on its way," comes the butler's languid voice from the archway that links the parlor to the front hall, making Ward start.

Turn to **173**.

124

"What have you done to them?" you demand, your gaze fixed on the bodies of the other guests.

"It is not my doing. It is the dreamers whose dreaming holds open the portal to the domain of the great Atlach-Nacha," Knott says calmly, as if he is telling you his breakfast details rather than spouting words that invite nothing but terror and insanity. "Mr Harcourt faces his apotheosis, when he shall join the Mother Goddess, she who weaves between worlds, Atlach-Nacha. All that needs to happen now is for the Key to open the Door."

It is through you that the Key shall turn – Harcourt wrote in his second letter to you – and the Door shall be opened.

"I am the Key?" you say, bewildered.

"Yes!" the butler replies in excitement.

"But why?"

"Because of all that you have seen. Just as the secret knowledge you possess is the key to unlocking the truth, you will unlock the Door that will usher in his apotheosis! I have witnessed it in my dreams."

You and Isabel are suddenly seized from behind as the two housemaids materialize from out of the shadows. It feels like there are more than two hands on you, impossible as that would be.

But you're not going to let yourself be taken so easily.

Make a struggle test. Roll one die and add your **COMBAT**. You may spend **1 RESOURCE** to roll two dice and pick the highest. If you have the {AGILE}, {FIGHTER}, or {SURVIVOR} Ability, add 1. What's the result?

> Total of 8 or more: turn to **149**.
> 7 or less: turn to **253**.

125

You do not want to remain in Harcourt House a moment longer. You are determined to get away from this horrible house full of spiders if it's the last thing you do!

Hurrying down the steps you set off at a trot along the drive. The red maples loom on either side of you through the mist, all of them smothered in spiderwebs. The trees themselves don't appear to look right, though. They seem to have become stranger and more fantastical than a red maple should be – the branches are thicker, with the leaves oddly shaped.

As your mind is puzzling over how so many trees can have metamorphosed and yet become completely covered in webs within a few hours, an answer presents itself to one of your questions.

There are things writhing in the trees – great, bulbous things. You can tell through the perception-warping mists that they are each far larger than a human being. They move about on long, stick-like limbs, that are disturbingly multi-jointed, with an unnatural grace. Take **+ 1 DOOM**.

Perhaps it would be better to remain inside Harcourt House after all.

> If you want to turn around and head back to the house, turn to **137**.
> If you want to press on, turn to **157**.

126

You dash toward the attic stairs, heart hammering, your legs ready to give out from under you. Behind you, you hear the rasp of chitin on wood as the Harcourt-spider comes after you. You throw yourself down the stairs, praying for even a sliver of a chance of escape.

A wet, clicking hiss echoes through the gloom. Then – *THWIP!* – something strikes your back, heavy as a thrown net.

Your scream of terror is cut short as the web tightens instantly, cold and clinging. You are yanked off your feet, slammed into the floor, and then dragged backward – at speed. Splinters tear at your clothes and skin as you're reeled in by the abomination.

You catch one last glimpse of the roof joists above, then nothing but legs. Too many legs.

The creature that was once Elijah Harcourt looms over you, a human face melded grotesquely to the swollen spider-body, mouth distended, fangs twitching. The last thing you hear, whispered through disfiguring mandibles is, *"Foooood!"*

And then, with a sudden crunch of bone and a splash of warmth, your head is severed cleanly from your body between its jaws.

Your body twitches once. Then the feeding begins.

SECRET: *Will You Walk Into My Parlor?*

The End.

My Dear Doctor,

What would you say if I were to tell you that there is a way to escape all of life's ills and never be troubled by ailment, agony or addiction ever again? Surely, the discovery of such a panacea must be the dream of every physician in the world.

But I do not need to tell you for you will see for yourself very soon. For all that you have done for me over the years I offer you release from further torment and anguish, for the time of ascension has come. This night, your dreams will be the making of us both. Ecstasy beyond imagining shall be ours. You have never tasted a drug like this!

Tonight, the Key will turn, the Door will open, and we will enter paradise together and say goodbye to all mortal infirmities and inadequacies.

Elijah Harcourt

Now turn to the number you were told to write down before reading the letter Elijah Harcourt wrote to Dr Harrow.

"What are you doing?" exclaims Varnum in disbelief.

"What I should have done already," you tell him. "Looking for the spider that has now claimed two victims, before it claims a third."

You scour the room, trying to think where the spider would be hiding now, having only just bitten Dr Bellweather.

Make a search test. Roll one die and add your **INTELLECT**. You may spend **1 CLUE** to roll two dice and pick the highest. If you have the {**SEEKER**} Ability, add 1. What's the result?

> Total of 7 or more: turn to **178**.
> 6 or less: turn to **239**.

The door suddenly opens, and Horace Trenholm pops his head into the room.

"Ah, Otto, there you are," he blusters. "Can I have a word?"

Smoothing the creases of his jacket, the professor says, "Of course, Horace. Is something the matter?"

"Not at all, not at all," Trenholm assures him with a too-hearty laugh, though his eyes flick briefly to you, appraising you before sliding away again. He jerks his head toward the corridor. "Just a trifling business. Won't take a moment. Best spoken of out here, eh?"

And with that, he withdraws, leaving the heavy door ajar,

the hush of the library pressing upon you more keenly in his absence.

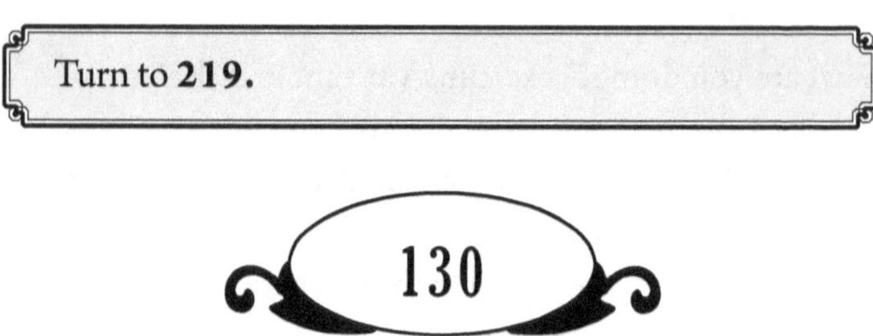

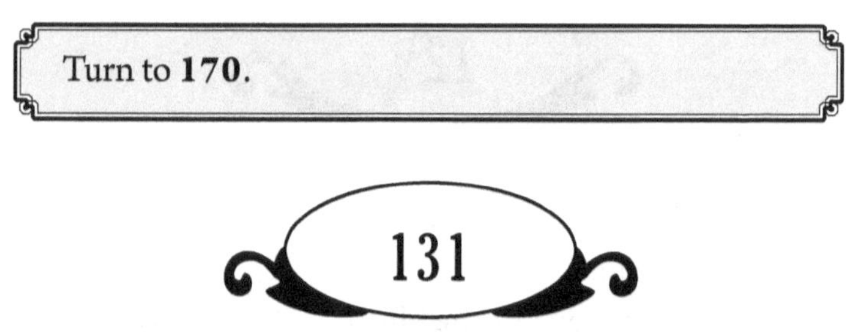

The longer you examine the photographs, the worse the illusory sensation becomes until you feel like it isn't just the images that are moving, but that the spiders have taken physical form and are scuttling about under the glass in the display case.

Take - **1 SANITY** and the SECRET: *Seeing Things.*

You can bear to remain here no longer and so leave without a moment's hesitation.

Turn to **170**.

131

Kingsport's Harborside forms a barrier between the sea, the periodically encroaching mists, and the main body of the town. Here are red brick warehouses, the rough edges smoothed by the salt sea air and moisture, the same weather conditions having cracked and splintered the wooden posts of the docks that proliferate the area.

Fishing boats rise and fall with the tide while their crews

mend nets and lobster pots on the dockside. When you mention the name Elijah Harcourt to some of them, all you receive in return are blank faces. Clearly, the man you are visiting moves in very different circles from the fisherfolk of the town.

Moving on, you skirt the harbor – with its ferry terminal and large, ocean-going passenger ships – coming at last to the North Port Lighthouse. The structure towers over the town and, since its recent refurbishment, it has become a popular destination for tourists.

You join a party of excitable sightseers in climbing to the top, where strong iron railings ensure everyone's safety whilst enjoying the views, and revel in the town's layout and its gorgeous surroundings. On the cliffs above Kingsport, you see several grand houses with neatly kept gardens. This neighborhood seems to be its own separate part of Kingsport, one much more reserved compared to the Harborside.

A young man with poor skin, whom you take to be a junior lighthouse keeper, is up there chaperoning both you and the other excited tourists, making sure no one comes to any harm and keeping an eye on those who might test the railings. Seeing you staring intently at the clifftop residences, he sidles over and says, "How the other half live, eh?"

"Quite," you say. "Are any of them Harcourt House?"

The junior lighthouse keeper looks uneasy. "You'll get a better view through this," he says, indicating a telescope mounted to the railings. "Just put a nickel in the slot."

Why not? you think and push in a coin. However, when you put your eye to the eyepiece all you can see through the viewing scope is a strange, purple-tinted mist. Looking away from the eyepiece, you note that everything was as it was before with only a periwinkle mist roping about the houses, groves, and gardens. When you peer through the telescope again, the view transitions once more – eerily amethyst-tinted and obscured.

"It's not working," you tell the young man. "The lens has been damaged."

"I can assure you it is in working order," he says, affronted. "Perhaps you're not using it properly."

You are about to argue but then decide you can't be bothered. As the junior lighthouse keeper wanders over to a pair of young women who have now made it to the top of the tower, you check the time and reluctantly decide to make the descent and end your tourist adventure.

You're not sure you're in the right part of town to find out more about Harcourt House and its owner. However, there is one place that is guaranteed to be a hotbed of local rumors and gossip – even in these times of supposed Prohibition.

> If you want to look for a local hostelry, in the hope that you will find what you are looking for there, turn to **47**.
>
> If not, turn to **150**.

132

Grabbing Dr Luther Harrow by the shoulders, you shake him violently while screaming in his face to wake up. His eyelids suddenly flick open, and he meets your gaze with a terrified stare. His eyes bulge out of his head as he opens his mouth and gives a bloodcurdling scream.

The scream is taken up by the other sleepers, who are also waking to the uncomfortable truth of the situation in which they now find themselves. And then the spider-thing squatting in the middle of the massive web starts to scream too, and you fear that your mind will break.

Roll one die.

> If the number rolled is equal to or less than your **SANITY**, turn to **176**.
> If the number rolled is greater than your **SANITY**, turn to **159**.

133

"I don't know who it could be," you reply.

"But that doesn't change the fact that there is a lunatic hiding in plain sight, somewhere in the house!" Isabel cries, her voice trembling with fear.

"It's all right, my dear," the attorney says, steering her to a chair and encouraging her to sit down. "Stay here. I won't be a moment."

And with that, he leaves the parlor.

You can't help thinking that if you are to get to the bottom of what's going on here, and find whoever it was that stabbed Professor Varnum, you would do better to keep exploring Harcourt House. But then again, perhaps Peregrine Ward is right, and it would make more sense to stay here in the parlor with Isabel. As they say, there is safety in numbers.

> If you want to explore the house, turn to **57**.
> If you want to remain in the parlor, turn to **77**.

134

"Does this house have an attic?" you ask Isabel.

She stares at you, befuddled. "Yes, of course. But what's that got to do with anything?"

"Because that must be where the spiders have taken Ward," you tell her. "How do we get up there?"

"Through the vestibule before the museum," she says, in a quiet voice.

"No," says Dr Harrow firmly. "We are not going up there. Did you see what those things did to him? To a full-grown man?"

"We all did," you bite back.

"No. We phone the authorities for help, and we stick together, no matter what!" the doctor states emphatically.

> If you want to go along with Dr Harrow's plan, turn to **152**.
> If you want to make your way to the attic, turn to **61**.
> If you want to go somewhere else, turn to **175**.

You have one purpose now: to bring an end to the blasphemous ambitions of Elijah Harcourt and the demonic deity to whom he has sworn his life, his being, and his very soul.

With Isabel Harcourt at your side, you prepare to battle the monster in its lair.

You may spend **1 RESOURCE** at the start of each round to add 2 to your total for that round.

Round one: roll two dice and add your **COMBAT** and your **WILLPOWER**. If you have the {AGILE}, {RESOLVED} or {SURVIVOR} Ability, add 1. If you have the Weakness {CAUTIOUS}, deduct 1. If the total is 14 or more, you win the first round.

Round two: roll two dice and add your **COMBAT** and your **WILLPOWER**. If you have the {FIGHTER} or {TOUGH} Ability, add 1. If you won the first round, add 2. If your total is 15 or more, you win the second round.

If you won the second round, turn to **113**.
If you lost the second round, turn to **153**.

"What do you think you are doing?" Ward exclaims in horror, as you snatch up the envelope.

"I am going to read the letter Elijah Harcourt wrote to Dr Bellweather," you pronounce, preparing to slip a finger under the seal and rip it open.

"I command you to stop!" he roars, and you suddenly know what it must be like to face him in a court of law. You understand why Elijah Harcourt employed Peregrine Ward to be his attorney; the sheer force of the man's domineering will is overwhelming.

Make a determination test. Roll one die and add your **WILLPOWER**. You may spend **1 RESOURCE** to roll two dice and pick the highest. You may add 1 to the dice roll if you have the {LEGAL KNOWLEDGE}, {MYSTIC} or {SORCERY} Ability. If you have the Weakness {CAUTIOUS}, deduct 1. What's the result?

> Total of 8 or more: turn to **196**.
> 7 or less: turn to **5**.

137

Icy dread courses through your veins as you turn and set off at a run back toward the house, not knowing what else to do. You feel the air shift above you, and then a great globular shape lands on the drive in front of you with a crunch of gravel, sending swirling eddies through the mist.

It looks like a colossal spider, but at the same time doesn't. Its limbs are multi-jointed and splayed, the body segmented in asymmetrical parts. The swollen abdomen is cloaked in gray chitin and it has multiple glowing eyes, looking like a cluster of boils on its head, ripe and ready to pop.

Take - **1 SANITY**.

> Turn to **218**.

138

Which item did you choose?

If it was a [BOOK OF MATCHES], a [GROTESQUE IDOL], a [LIGHTER], or a [POTTERY SHARD], turn to 151.
If it was something else, turn to 49.

139

You're not sure precisely what it was you were hoping to discover by returning to the study, but examining the huge mahogany desk certainly doesn't provide you with any new information. In fact, it feels like you are wasting time by searching this room again. Take -1 CLUE and -1 INTELLECT.

Turn to 289.

140

The library of Harcourt House is an impressive repository of very specialist knowledge relating to all things Arachnida.

> If you have a [SHIRT BUTTON], turn to **282**.
> If not, but you have some [PINCE-NEZ GLASSES], turn to **10**.
> If not, but you have a [FOSSIL FANG], turn to **96**.
> If you do not have any of the above items, turn to **162**.

141

Under the horror's relentless assault, you fall to the floor, and the mummified corpse then falls on top of you. Its dusty eye sockets and rictus grin mere inches from your face, the abomination continues to shake and shudder as it lies on top of you until it comes apart, a multitude of hairy black bodies spilling from within the cage of dry bones and tearing, parchment skin.

You cry out in pain as one of the spiders sinks its fangs into your cheek. The onslaught doesn't stop as more of the arachnids bite you until their combined venom overcomes you and you lose consciousness.

As a result, you remain ignorant of your fate, which is probably for the best.

SECRET: *Once Bitten.*

The End.

The handle rattles loosely as you open the door and enter Harcourt's private museum.

> If you have a [**POTTERY SHARD**], turn to **25**.
> If not, turn to **54**.

The letters – at least, you assume they are letters – are all in sealed envelopes and addressed in the same spidery hand as your invitation to Kingsport. You recognize it at once as Elijah Harcourt's handwriting.

"There's one addressed to each of us," says Isabel Harcourt, suddenly at your shoulder.

"We should give them out," you say. "Then perhaps we'll know why your uncle summoned everyone here this evening in the first place."

"I agree," says Isabel, stacking the envelopes into a neat pile before taking them in hand and marching out of the study, back to the parlor.

You follow.

> Turn to **173**.

144

To your left, beyond a small vestibule, is a polished walnut door bearing the sign "Museum."

If you want to open the door and enter the museum, turn to **142**.
If not, turn to **94**.

145

The library doubtless has much more to teach you, but you know it is not the only room in the house to contain mysterious secrets.

So, what do you want to do?

Examine [**FORGOTTEN CULTS OF HYPERBOREA**]: turn to **201**.
Take a look at [**OLDE KINGSPORT AND ITS CURIOSITIES**]: turn to **232**.
Study [**THE SOMNAMBULIST'S PATH**]: turn to **180**.
Leave and go somewhere else: turn to **140**.

Along with the usual accoutrements you would expect to find in a doctor's bag – stethoscope, sphygmomanometer, thermometer, auriscope, and reflex hammer – you find a syringe that looks like it has been used recently, due to the small amount of blood-laced solution still in the barrel, and a half-empty vial of morphine.

However, as you turn the bottle around in your hand, you notice a few milky streaks within the liquid. Is it unadulterated morphine that is contained within the glass vial, or has it been contaminated by the introduction of something else?

Take **+1 CLUE, +2 RESOURCES, +1 INTELLECT**, and record the [**SYRINGE OF MORPHINE**] on your Character Sheet.

However, that is not all that is in the bag. You also find a letter addressed to Dr Luther Harrow written in Elijah Harcourt's distinctive, spidery hand.

If you want to read the letter, make a note of the number **107** on your Character Sheet and then turn to **127** to read the letter.

If you feel that you don't have the luxury of taking the time required to read the letter now, turn to **107** right away.

"Oh, just a lot of vindictive rubbish, threats and the like," the explorer says dismissively, "but look who's laughing now."

He takes a swig from the hip flask. Trenholm doesn't seem to be in a particular jolly mood to you.

He chuckles humorlessly. "Not Otto, that's for sure."

Did any of the people invited to Harcourt House this evening actually like each other? You feel even more strongly than before that you are going to need to keep your wits about you. Take **+1 WILLPOWER**.

If you want to ask him who he thinks could have attacked Professor Varnum, turn to **217**.
If you are done interrogating the explorer, turn to **257**.

Elijah Harcourt is not alone. Dr Luther Harrow is there with him. He has his back turned to you and appears to be searching for something in his medical bag, which is resting on the bedside table. "It will be better soon," he whispers.

Harcourt is lying on his back, and you can see that his face is covered with a livid purple tracery that emanates from the bite on his neck, which itself is now a swollen red and yellow mass the size of your fist.

Seeing him like this, you give an involuntary gasp. Dr Harrow spins around with a start. In his hand is a syringe, a droplet of moisture glistening at its tip. What is he doing?

If you want to quickly back out of the room, turn to **182**.

If you want to challenge Dr Harrow, turn to **231**.

If you fear he is up to no good and want to strike before he can do Elijah Harcourt further harm, turn to **21**.

149

You manage to break the young woman's hold on you, taking her, the other maid, and Knott all by surprise and giving Isabel the distraction she needs to break free of her captor.

"You dare defy the will of Atlach-Nacha?" the butler cries. "You can struggle all you like but the master will feast on your defiance!"

You say nothing in reply. The time for talking is done, for you know that you are now fighting for your life.

You lead the charge while Isabel, following your lead, joins you in battling the servants in order to escape the horrors of Harcourt House.

You may spend **1 RESOURCE** at the start of each round to add 2 to your total for that round.

Round one: roll two dice and add your **COMBAT**. If you have the {**FIGHTER**} Ability, add 1. If you have the

Weakness {CAUTIOUS}, deduct 1. If the total is 12 or more, you win the first round.

Round two: roll two dice and add your **COMBAT**. If you have the {TOUGH} Ability, add 1. If you won the first round, add 1. If your total is 16 or more, you win the second round.

Round three: roll two dice and add your **COMBAT**. If you have the {SURVIVOR} Ability, add 1. And if you won the second round, add 2. If your total is 17 or more, you win the third round.

> If you won all three rounds, turn to **221**.
> If you won two rounds, turn to **205**.
> If you lost two rounds, turn to **185**.
> If you lost all three rounds, turn to **168**.

150

You are intrigued as to why Elijah Harcourt was so emphatic in his letter that you should arrive at his home at 7 PM. You certainly don't want to be late, so you look for a cab to take you there.

Fortunately, your search doesn't take long, and soon you are leaving the district, bouncing along a tarmacked road that zigzags left and right as it heads up to the cliffs that loom over Kingsport.

Pulling up outside a set of blackened iron gates, your driver announces that this is the place. Harcourt House. As you step out, he glances at the large mansion with a flicker of unease. "Not many folk go there and with good reason," he mutters quietly. "Old Harcourt House – plenty of stories, none that would do you much good."

Unsettled by the comment, you nod but say nothing else. After you've paid the fare, the cabbie revs the engine and peels away without asking if you'll want picking up again later.

You watch the departing automobile, noting how a thin mist has begun creeping up the road toward the house. With a shudder, you turn to push open the gates of Harcourt House, and you make your way along the graveled driveway that leads to the white-walled mansion sitting between an avenue of evenly spaced red maple trees. The atmosphere is calm and solemn. As your shoes crunch the gravel beneath them, the mist drifts across the well-kept lawns as if with a mind of its own, softening the edges of the mansion's white walls as it gathers in slow-moving wispy curls.

Climbing the steps to the porch, you ring the bell. A few moments later the great black lacquered door opens, and a butler – a short but stocky man with a sallow complexion, his dark hair slicked back with a generous application of pomade – admits you to the house just as a grandfather clock somewhere within marks the time with seven chimes. Behind him, a pair of housemaids make themselves scarce.

From the expansive front hall, the butler – who you think must be in his fifties – guides you into the parlor where you find six other guests already gathered. There are four men and two women, and they all regard you with judgment and suspicion apart from a tall, gaunt African-American gentleman, impeccably dressed in a well-tailored gray suit. He steps forward and offers you his hand whilst peering down at you through the pince-nez glasses perched on the end of his nose.

"Peregrine Ward," he says, shaking your hand firmly. "Personal attorney to Mr Harcourt. And you are?"

You introduce yourself and Ward then takes it upon himself to formally introduce you to everyone else present.

The first is a young woman in her twenties, Isabel Harcourt, your host's niece. Pale, with angular features, and her dark hair worn in a fashionable bob, the dress she is wearing is modest but elegant, although you detect subtle hints of rebellion in her attire – namely the scarlet scarf wrapped loosely around her neck, and the cigarette holder she has balanced between the index and middle fingers of her right hand.

Next is Professor Otto Varnum, who is a complete contrast to Miss Harcourt in every way. Heavyset with thinning gray hair and deep-set eyes, his tweed three-piece suit is outdated and screams academia, as does the faint smell of dust and old books that seems to hang about him. You are not surprised to learn that he is a historian with a lecturer position at Miskatonic University in Arkham.

A rugged and suntanned man steps forward to make your acquaintance, bypassing the diminutive, bespectacled Hispanic woman you thought you were going to meet next.

"Horace Trenholm," he says, trapping your hand in a crushing callused grip. "Explorer and adventurer." Certainly, the weather-beaten leather jacket he is wearing and the bulging satchel he carries over one shoulder would attest to that, as do his rough beard and sharp eyes.

Where Trenholm is possessed of a confident swagger, the bespectacled woman radiates social awkwardness and blushes when the two of you are introduced. She struggles to maintain eye contact, her gaze continually straying to the toes of her sensible shoes. Short, wiry, and with round spectacles perched on her nose, she is wearing a purple buttoned cardigan and a long gray skirt.

"Dr Cora Bellweather," she says, "zoologist, with a particular interest in Arachnida."

Last is a man in his mid-forties. Everything about him gives the impression that he is a once-successful individual for whom things have not gone so well of late. Clearly once handsome, his appearance is now haggard, with sunken eyes and a ghostly complexion. Likewise, his suit is clearly tailored but it, too, has seen better days.

"This is Dr Luther Harrow," Ward announces, "Mr Harcourt's personal physician."

"Pleased to meet you," Harrow replies.

As you shake the doctor's hand, do you detect a slight tremor? You wonder why someone like a qualified doctor would need to feel nervous in such company. He seems to be almost as socially awkward as Dr Bellweather and looks like he stopped taking care of himself a long time ago. You only hope he takes better care of his patients.

"How much longer are we going to have to wait, Knott?" Ward asks the butler, who is hovering just outside the parlor in the hall.

"Mr Harcourt will be ready for you shortly," the butler replies somberly.

Having summarily introduced you to everybody, Ward takes Isabel Harcourt by the arm and leads her to a corner of the room, where the two are soon engaged in an intense whispered conversation.

Professor Varnum sidles over to a drinks trolley to refill his whiskey glass. Dr Harrow joins him there, leaving Trenholm and Dr Bellweather together in the middle of the room.

Still wondering why you have been summoned to this gathering, and preferring not to be excluded from the group, you decide to impose yourself upon one of the pairs. But which is it to be?

Peregrine Ward and Isabel Harcourt: turn to **120**.
Professor Varnum and Dr Harrow: turn to **220**.
Horace Trenholm and Dr Bellweather: turn to **190**.

The spiders fall from you onto the floor and scuttle away, disappearing between the banisters, under pieces of furniture, and running back up the walls to rejoin the rest of the swarm.

However, you also receive a few painful bites. Take -1 **HEALTH**.

Turn to **100**.

"Do you know where the telephone is kept?" you ask.

"Out back under the stairs, in the servants' passage on the way to the kitchen, I believe," Dr Harrow says, already leading the way there, with you and Isabel Harcourt following close on his heels.

He is right. It is a candlestick telephone and stands on a shelf in its own cubbyhole. Picking up the receiver, Dr Harrow dials zero for the operator and prepares to speak into the mouthpiece.

"Hello?" he says, anxiously. "Can you hear me? Hello! Is there anybody there?"

You meet Isabel's anxious stare.

"There's no signal. No dial tone, nothing!" Dr Harrow sounds bewildered.

"Let me try," you say, taking the receiver from him and pushing him aside. But he's right, the telephone is dead.

And then your eyes stray to the cord that should be connected to the telephone jack in the wall. It has been pulled out of the socket, the exposed wires telling you all you need to know. Someone sabotaged the telephone.

But who could have done such a thing and why? Your mind racing, you start to wonder, did Knott even call for help at all?

You can't bear to stand here and do nothing as the situation steadily goes from bad to worse, so you set off to look for the butler and have it out with him.

Turn to **296**.

153

The spider-thing looms over you, opening its mouth again. This time, its jaws distend in ways that defy nature and human physiology. The vile stench of its insides makes you gag as it lowers its head, enclosing yours between those monstrous fangs.

With one swift bite, it ends your misery.

Secret: *Bite Me!*

The End.

You suddenly have a vision of a monstrous spider, not at the heart of the desert but in a cave, deep underground. It is attended by other spiders that you somehow know are huge, but that are still dwarfed by their queen.

While the vision is unsettling, you feel that to be forewarned is to be forearmed.

Take +**1** **SANITY**, +**1** **WILLPOWER**, and the SECRET: *Hidden Four.*

> Now turn back to **73**.

While the study shelves are crammed with all manner of items, the desk is spotlessly tidy, with a place for everything and everything in its place, including the fountain pens and inkwell in a stand on the desk.

> If you have a [**FULL SPECIMEN JAR**], turn to **55**.
> If not, turn to **285**.

156

As you close the door again, Isabel offers you a concerned smile.

You can't bear to stand around doing nothing, so where do you want to go now?

To visit the study again, turn to **17**.
To visit the library, turn to **181**.
To visit the museum, turn to **142**.
To visit the recently revealed secret room behind the bookcase, turn to **74**.
To visit Elijah Harcourt's bedroom to see how your host is faring, turn to **62**.

157

Desperation drives you on, and you pick up the pace. You have no idea whether the things in the trees adhere to any sort of territory or boundary. Will it make any difference if you manage to leave the grounds? You have to try!

But as you keep sprinting down the drive, the creatures start to close in, descending silently from the trees and racing with jerky steps toward you across the grass.

If you want to use something from among your possessions to fend them off, turn to **179**.
If not, or you don't think you have anything that would be of use in the current situation, turn to **218**.

158

Dr Harrow warily enters the study again, accompanied by Trenholm, but you hang back with the others. While all eyes, including yours, are on what is going on within, Professor Varnum sidles over to you and says in a low voice only you can hear, "Do you think she had something to do with it?"

"With what happened to Elijah? But it was an accident, wasn't it?" you ask.

Professor Varnum gives you a pointed look. "Was it?"

If you are in possession of an [EMPTY GLASS JAR], turn to **264**.
If not, turn to **178**.

And then another voice joins the cacophony, but it takes a moment for you to realize it is your own. All that you have witnessed and endured this night in the house of spiders has taken an irredeemable toll on your mind, driving you to the brink of madness.

You fall to your knees on the unfinished floorboards, every ounce of fight gone out of you.

The spider-thing looms over you, opening its mouth again. This time, its jaws distend in ways that defy nature and human physiology. The vile stench of its insides makes you gag as it lowers its head, enclosing yours between those monstrous fangs. With one swift bite, it ends your misery.

The End.

A thought suddenly strikes you. The many-armed statuette clearly has some connection to one of the many spider cults that worship Atlach-Nacha, the spinner in darkness, in various forms around the world. As a result, it may be imbued with power and so you take it out and brandish it before you.

In an instant, the spiders freeze. You were right! Take +1 INTELLECT, -1 DOOM, and the SECRET: *Hidden Six.*

Sweeping the idol from left to right and back again, the hundreds of spiders actually start to retreat before you.

Turn to **24.**

You take off his tie and loosen his collar, and then, taking a steadying breath, you gently pat down his clothes to make sure that there's nothing furry and eight-legged hiding out of sight within. Having convinced yourself that he isn't harboring any unwanted stowaways, you check any exposed skin – his face, neck and hands – for signs that he has been bitten but find nothing.

That is, until you roll up his shirt sleeves – the cuffs having already been rolled back to expose his wrists, thereby making it more comfortable for him when carrying out patient examinations – and see the tiny puncture marks that cover his inner left forearm. You're startled and worried but then you peer closer.

These are not the marks left by dozens of spider bites. Some are scabbed over and many are surrounded by old bruises. There is no doubt in your mind that they are track marks, the legacy of numerous and frequent injections by hypodermic needle.

Could Dr Harrow himself be responsible for his current condition? Take +**1 CLUE**.

> If you now want to check his doctor's bag, turn to **146**.
>
> If you want to see if Knott has been able to call for help, turn to **107**.

162

An anguished cry suddenly carries to you from somewhere upstairs. You can't be sure, but it sounded like a man.

Hurrying up the stairs, you arrive at the top as Dr Harrow is approaching across the landing from the right.

"Did you see that?" he says. "I thought I saw someone run into the vestibule in front of Harcourt's museum."

"You're the first person I've seen since coming upstairs," you tell him.

You are standing in front of an alcove in which stands a bookcase and a reading chair, set beneath a window that looks out over the grounds to the east. However, the bookcase appears to have been pulled forward so that it is almost entirely blocking the entrance to the reading nook, and it is only as you draw closer that you realize it is actually part of a secret door – one that is currently being held open by a body. The faint glow of an electric light comes from the room that lies beyond it.

You and Dr Harrow converge on the spot at the same time, and you see that it is Otto Varnum who is holding the hidden door open. He is lying on his left side, with his back to you.

"Not another one," hisses Dr Harrow as he bends down to assess the condition of his latest patient.

"What's happened?" Horace Trenholm demands as he arrives on the scene, clearly having followed you up the stairs.

Turn to **85**.

You find nothing of interest on the floor, but you keep thinking you can see things moving at the periphery of your vision. When you turn your head to catch what it is you think you see, there is nothing there. But then, the scuttling shadows have moved to the corners of your eyes once more and remain always just out of sight. Take -**1 SANITY**.

If you have a [SHIRT BUTTON], turn to **282**.
If not, but you have some [PINCE-NEZ GLASSES], turn to **10**.
If not, but you have a [FOSSIL FANG], turn to **96**.
If you do not have any of the above items, turn to **162**.

When you are sure the coast is clear, you creep upstairs, keeping to the shadows as much as you can, and soon reach the second-floor landing.

If you have a [FOSSIL FANG], turn to **114**.
If not, turn to **144**.

Decoding the script, you start to intone what you hope is a magical spell. But the mere presence of the horror that was Elijah Harcourt, and the distressing condition of the sleepers, are a constant distraction to your beleaguered sensibilities.

Make a concentration test. Roll one die and add your **WILLPOWER**. You may spend **1 RESOURCE** to roll two dice and pick the highest. If you have the Weakness {**ARACHNOPHOBIA**}, deduct 1. If you have the {**MYSTIC**}, {**SECRET RITES**}, or {**STUDIOUS**} Ability, add 1. If you have the {**ARCANE STUDIES**} or {**SORCERY**} Ability, add 2. What's the result?

Total of 10 or more: turn to **300**.
9 or less: turn to **281**.

"Would you like to share what Elijah wrote to you with the group?" Ward challenges Trenholm.

"No, I would not," comes the explorer's blunt response. "But I suspect you already know what was in it, considering you're his personal attorney."

"I can assure you that I didn't even know Mr Harcourt was writing those letters, let alone what they were about."

"Oh, is that so? But you knew he hadn't paid me for that last lot of artifacts I brought back for him from South America? You manage all his financial affairs as well, right?"

You notice a slight blush in Ward's cheeks then, but whether it is a sign of guilt, embarrassment, anger, or the effects of the brandy, you cannot be sure.

Your interest has been piqued, but you're not sure whether to risk goading either the explorer or the attorney with your own questions or remain a silent observer to their exchange.

What do you want to do?

> Pick up on Trenholm's comment about monies owed: turn to **236**.
>
> Ask Ward if he really does manage Elijah Harcourt's affairs: turn to **266**.
>
> Say nothing: turn to **273**.

167

The bedside reading lamp shines a soft light, but there is nothing of interest on the small table. However, opening the drawer beneath it, you find a [BOOK OF MATCHES]. You presume they are kept there in case of a power outage, or perhaps to indulge in a pipe.

If you want to take the [BOOK OF MATCHES], record it on your Character Sheet and take +1 RESOURCE.

> Turn to **276**.

Despite your resistance being driven by desperation, Knott and the housemaids are driven by a zealous fanaticism, and maybe something more – something beyond human emotion. And, unfortunately, Isabel is no fighter.

Your body beaten and your desire to resist broken, the resilient housemaids seize hold of both of you again, while the butler prepares to carry out his final duty for Elijah Harcourt.

Turn to **270**.

Varnum's voice is little more than a whisper, his words barely audible, but you can at least partially make out what he is saying.

"There were three of us once… I always wondered what happened to Toby… I suspect he never left… after he argued with Elijah."

Take + **1 CLUE** and the SECRET: *The Three Amigos.*

Turn to **209**.

Not for the first time, you find yourself wondering why you ever gave in to your overwhelming sense of curiosity and decided to visit Harcourt House this night.

If you have a [SHIRT BUTTON], turn to 282.
If not, but you have some [PINCE-NEZ GLASSES], turn to 202.
If not, but you have a [FOSSIL FANG], turn to 192.
If you do not have any of the above items, turn to 39.

You have never seen so many spider-related treasures and totems. As well as the obsidian spider, the banner, and the weights, there are also Japanese netsuke – tiny, carved toggles – featuring spiders in their design. The carving of some of the objects reflects the myriad cultures from which the items must have been collected. An ebony mask with extremely stylized features puts you in mind of wood carvings from West Africa, while some of the pieces are so crude that you could easily believe they date from as far back as the Neolithic.

However, your attention is particularly drawn to a photograph that is propped up against a vase. It is a picture of a statuette that vaguely reminds you of the statuary of the Indian subcontinent. It takes the form of an eight-armed goddess but her otherwise appealing face has been distorted by the addition of a great pair of fangs. Take **+1 CLUE**.

> Turn to **289**.

172

With one final herculean effort you stand before the web, but face to face with the abomination you are frozen to the spot by sheer terror.

"Foooood," the creature says with something like hideous delight.

Opening its malformed mouth, it lurches toward you and sinks its fangs into your hip and side. Take **-2 HEALTH** and **-1 COMBAT**.

Roll one die and deduct 1 if you have the {**SURVIVOR**} or {**TOUGH**} Ability.

> If the total is equal to or less than your **HEALTH**, turn to **135**.
> If the total is greater than your **HEALTH**, turn to **153**.

Once Dr Harrow has completed his examination, he asks the guests to gather in the parlor.

"How is he?" asks Isabel. "How's my uncle?"

"Still unconscious," replies the doctor, "but the household staff are taking turns to check in on him, as will I."

"Was his condition caused by a spider bite?" asks Peregrine Ward.

"Of that I am certain," says the doctor. He hesitates, scanning the faces of the people in the room. "Where's Dr Bellweather?"

"Last time I saw her, she was searching for the spider in Harcourt's study," you say.

At that moment, Knott the butler appears at Dr Harrow's shoulder.

"Is help on the way?" asks the doctor.

"Yes," replies Knott, "medical assistance will arrive shortly."

"How long until it's here?" Professor Varnum asks.

"Within the hour," says Knott.

"So, what are we supposed to do while we wait?" asks Trenholm.

"We could find out why my uncle summoned us all here," Isabel says, holding up the wad of sealed envelopes that were on the desk in Harcourt's study. "I mean, I would imagine that's what these contain – an answer. There's one addressed to each of us."

"But why gather everyone here on this night in particular?" you ask.

"If we open our letters, maybe we'll find out."

Ward gives a heavy sigh. "Very well."

"Let me, Miss Harcourt," says Knott, and she automatically hands them to the butler.

The butler distributes the letters, reading out each recipient's name in turn. When he reads out your name, you take the envelope and retreat to a corner of the room.

The parlor goes quiet as everyone reads their letter from Elijah Harcourt. You cannot help noticing how the others shoot each other shifty glances, and you are reminded, not for the first time this evening, that you are the outsider here. At least some of them knew each other prior to gathering at the house on this night.

> You may read your letter at any time. Whenever you wish to read the letter, you should make a note of the section you are on at the time and then turn to **216**.
>
> However, now turn to **20**.

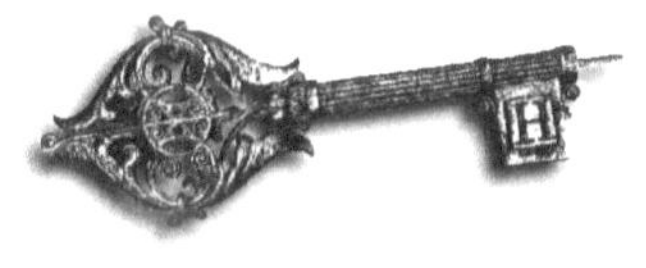

174

You are starting to believe that your situation is hopeless and that there is nothing you can do to alter the fate that the universe has prepared for you.

Take -**1 SANITY** and +**1 DOOM**.

Roll one die. If you have the Weakness {FEAR OF INSECTS}, add 1. If you have the Weakness {TROUBLED DREAMS}, add 1. And, if you have the Weakness {ARACHNOPHOBIA}, add 2.

> If the total is equal to or less than your **SANITY**, turn to **69**.
>
> If the total is greater than your **SANITY**, turn to **26**.

175

Deciding it would be wise not to rely on anyone else in this treacherous place, you set off alone in search of answers.

But where do you want to go?

> The study: turn to **41**.
>
> The library: turn to **181**.
>
> The museum: turn to **142**.
>
> The secret room hidden behind the bookcase: turn to **74**.
>
> If you want to check on Elijah Harcourt, turn to **62**.
>
> If you want to check on Dr Harrow's other patients, who have been put in the guest bedrooms, turn to **214**.
>
> Alternatively, if you want to leave the house after all, turn to **91**.

You have to escape this place of madness!

You run for the exit, pulling Isabel after you. Neither of you dares to look back – not even once – as you rush down the creaky stairs, taking them two at a time. Reaching the second-floor landing, you race for the central staircase and upon reaching the front hall, throw open the door and head out into the night.

But the pernicious mist that has surrounded Harcourt House since you arrived appears to be dissipating at last. You and Isabel sprint down the drive, through the gates, and away down the road toward the town that lies below the cliffs.

You and Isabel might have escaped with your lives, but Harcourt House still stands. Not only that, but Elijah Harcourt has achieved what he set out to do, having broken free of his mortal, human form to become like his blasphemous deity. And who knows what will happen to your fellow guests now?

Take -**1** **SANITY**, +**1** **DOOM**, and the SECRET: *A Fate Worse Than Death.*

Final score: 1 star.

The End.

It must have taken years – decades even – to build up such a collection, not to mention a lot of cold, hard cash.

If you have a [FOSSIL FANG], turn to **203**.
If not, turn to **234**.

And then, out of the corner of your eye, you see something scuttle out from under the desk. It looks like a ball of black and red wool, traveling across the carpet on eight legs that move with an eerie rippling motion. The creature is heading toward the shadows that lurk beneath one of the bookcases in the study.

If only you had something you could trap it with!

> If you are in possession of an
> [EMPTY GLASS JAR], turn to **198**.
> If not, turn to **6**.

What do you have that you think could help keep the approaching spider-things at bay?

> A [FLASHLIGHT]: turn to **9**.
> A [LIGHTER] or a
> [BOOK OF MATCHES]: turn to **260**.
> A [POTTERY SHARD] or a
> [GROTESQUE IDOL]: turn to **101**.
> If you do not have any of these items, turn to **137**.

180

The Somnambulist's Path is a slender volume bound in pale leather. The prose within is fragmented, alternating between cryptic instructions, descriptions of dream-visions, and philosophical musings. Its unnamed author also claims sections are transcribed from older dream-manuscripts.

The book asserts that sleepwalking is not a malady but, in fact, the soul striving to reach the Dreamlands. But this is merely the first step on the path. It describes breathing exercises, symbolic gestures and stranger things like whispered invocations that supposedly weaken the tether between the body and the dreaming soul. Some passages even suggest using narcotics such as laudanum to achieve the state required to take the next step on the path. The author paints the Dreamlands not as a fantastical realm but an inverted double of waking reality – more mutable and more treacherous, but also a source of secret knowledge.

Take +**1** **CLUE**, gain the Ability {**STUDIOUS**}, and if you want to take the book with you, record [**THE SOMNAMBULIST'S PATH**] on your Character Sheet.

Turn to **140**.

The library is located in the northeast corner of Harcourt House, beyond the parlor and past the stairs to the second floor.

The walls are lined with built-in bookcases of dark wood and the two windows have curtains drawn against the night.

> If you are in possession of a [LEATHER BOOKMARK], turn to **228**.
> If not, turn to **200**.

A sudden, horrible cry from somewhere nearby causes you to hurry out of the room. You can't be sure, but you think it sounded like Professor Varnum.

With the banister to your left, you see a shadowy figure fleeing the landing as you arrive. What has happened?

You consider giving chase, but your attention is soon taken by what appears to be a startling rearrangement of the furniture on the landing.

Opposite the top of the stairs is the alcove that you barely registered before, so unremarkable was it. Within it stands a bookcase and a reading chair set beneath a window that looks out over the grounds of the house to the east.

However, your eye is drawn to it now since the bookcase appears to have been pulled forward so that it is almost entirely blocking the entrance to the reading nook. It is only as you draw closer that you realize the bookcase, in fact, forms a secret door – one that is currently being held open by a body. The faint glow of an electric light comes from the room that lies beyond it.

Drawing closer, you see that it is Otto Varnum who props the bookcase-door open. He is lying on his left side with his back to you.

"Not another one," hisses Dr Harrow from behind you, having followed you from Harcourt's bedchamber.

Turn to **85**.

183

You scour the immediate surrounding area, including under and around the wingback chair the doctor is sitting on, but find nothing. You only hope this doesn't mean there's a spider hiding somewhere inside his clothes.

Time is not on your side, so you need to decide what you want to do next and fast. Take - **1 INTELLECT**.

If you want to examine Harrow himself, just in case, turn to **161**.

If you want to check the contents of his doctor's bag, turn to **146**.

If you want to see if Knott has had any success, turn to **107**.

"Let me help," you say to Dr Harrow.

"There is no need to trouble yourself," interrupts Knott, suddenly there at your shoulder. "I will arrange for the servants to make Dr Bellweather comfortable upstairs."

You are slightly taken aback but Knott is insistent.

As the butler arranges for the servants to carry the unconscious arachnologist upstairs, you find yourself wondering how Elijah Harcourt is faring. You could wait and then follow the housemaids upstairs and look in on Harcourt while the others are preoccupied with Dr Bellweather.

> If you want to follow this course of action, turn to **164**.
>
> If you would rather follow Horace Trenholm into the parlor: turn to **76**.
>
> If you would rather join Isabel Harcourt in the hall: turn to **248**.

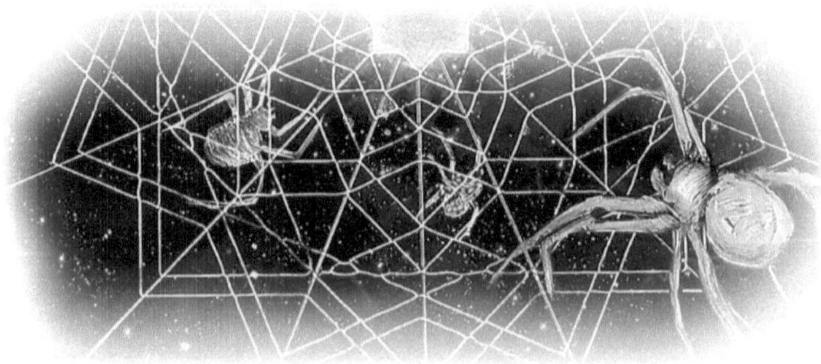

185

Things have gone from bad to worse as you have peeled away the layers of secrets contained within the house of spiders, until the ultimate horrific truth has been revealed to you.

Make a fate test. Roll one die, and if you have the Weakness {CURSED} or {TROUBLED DREAMS}, deduct 1.

> If the result is equal to or lower than the current **DOOM** level, turn to **168.**
> If the result is higher than the current **DOOM** level, turn to **205.**

186

Shaking off Isabel's hand you descend the steps to the gravel drive. The young woman watches from the door but does not leave the building to stop you. And so, you set off to look for help. Take + **1 WILLPOWER** and the SECRET: *Determined.*

The avenue of trees is barely visible through the all-consuming fog. In fact, it destroys any detail so that you could almost believe it had devoured the gardens and surrounding woodland, leaving nothing behind but an indistinct, lifeless grayness.

It is dark, but moonlight permeates the mist, giving it an eerie luminosity, despite your inability to see anything through it.

You calculate the end of the drive is only a five-minute walk away at most, but when twice that time has passed, or so you believe, there is still no sign of the corroded iron gates.

Starting to feel anxious, you convince yourself that the mist has distorted your perception of the passage of time as well as your visual acuity, and that the gates cannot be far away.

But after another ten minutes have passed, your pulse quickens as you begin to panic. Can you have gone the wrong way, somehow? Perhaps you passed the gates without realizing it, so preoccupied are you with everything that has happened since you arrived at Harcourt House.

You consider turning back or turning off the path you are following.

It is only then that you realize you cannot hear the crunch of gravel under the soles of your shoes. You look down, unease creeping along your spine. The mist is so thick, it's even hard to see your feet clearly. However, through the permeating moonlight you are just able to see that you are, in fact, walking along a muddy path. Your shoes are filthy!

Record the [DIRTY SHOES] on your Character Sheet if you haven't already done so.

In a complete panic now, you start to run before coming to your senses. A muddy track could mean you are following a precipitous path along the cliff top of Kingsport Head, with a hundred-foot drop to your left, invisible through the night and the fog.

You wonder if anyone will come to look for you. You wonder if you might fall to your death before that can happen. You wonder if you should stay where you are until the mist clears or turn around and go back the way you have come or press on. You wonder about all your options in the hours that pass while you remain lost in the mist.

Turn to **3**.

186

The drawers are filled with neatly pressed and folded shirts, monogrammed handkerchiefs, socks and items of underwear, precisely the sort of thing you would expect to find in a chest of drawers such as this. Despite your rummaging, you find nothing of interest nor anything that might help you get to the bottom of what is going on in Harcourt House.

Turn to **276.**

The first thing you notice about the hidden room is that it doesn't have any windows. There is an unmade safari camp-bed, a folding table and chair, and the door to what you imagine is a cupboard on the other side of the room.

Standing on the table is a [SILVER HIP FLASK]. Picking it up, you give it a shake and hear the slosh of liquid inside. Unscrewing the cap you take a sniff, your nostrils flaring and your eyes watering at the smell of the strong liquor within.

Record the [SILVER HIP FLASK] on your Character Sheet and take +1 RESOURCE.

As you look at the walls, you are amazed to see that maps

and pictures cover every inch of space, and even the cupboard
door.

> To study the maps and pictures, turn to **210**.
> To take a closer look at the bed and desk, turn to **230**.
> To open the cupboard and see what's inside, turn to **286**.
> If you want to leave the room, turn to **19**.

189

Leaning in close, you listen as Varnum spills his confession, his eyes wide and terrified.

"I had to know what happened to Toby," he says, his voice anxious as if he might be on his deathbed. "There were three of us to begin with, you see. Then one day there were just two of us. I always wondered what happened to Toby after he argued with Elijah, but I suspect he never left."

His eyelids flutter and close, and you fear he is about to lose consciousness.

"Toby who?" you ask.

The professor's eyes half open again. "Jugg… Toby Jugg… It's all in here." He pats the breast of his tweed jacket. "Read it and you'll understand."

His arm suddenly goes limp and flops to the floor next to him and his eyes close again. Dr Harrow swears and continues to administer aid to the professor.

Pulling open Varnum's jacket you find the letter Elijah had

written him tucked into the breast pocket. Taking it out, you read it.

My Dear Otto,

How long it has been since last we spoke without bitterness poisoning our words! Once, you and I were as twin stars set in a single firmament. I remember the nights when we were inseparable – not merely colleagues, but confidants, conspirators sharing a bond more intimate than scholarship dares confess. Yet time and pride have made strangers of us, and you have let the silence grow thick between us, like webs in a dusty attic.

You will recall, of course, the name we spoke together in candlelight, the patterns we traced, trembling, in chalk, when first we brushed against the hidden skeins of the Mother Goddess. But where I was ready to take that next vital step, you recoiled, calling what we had uncovered an abomination. But, in truth, it was a revelation. What you called blasphemy, I saw for what it was – inevitability. A weaving that was started long before either of us ever drew breath.

You were not the only one, of course, but you need not trouble yourself with idle speculation concerning the fate of dear Toby Jugg. Just know that he proved uncooperative. His night journeys to the Dreamlands haunted him during his waking hours, which in turn had kindled in him a reckless defiance. He and I argued, you know that. Otto, our last argument was truly terrible, too; however, you and I shared a bond that can never be broken. Jugg did not. And besides, he had already played his part, whereas you still have yours to perform.

What, did you think yourself spared? That by clinging to your scruples, you might remain beyond reach of that

*sublime glory we began? No. Your refusal does not free
you. It only binds you more tightly. The weaving requires
both of us, as it always has, and I have prepared the way.
When the Key turns and the Door yawns wide, you will
be there with me. My dreams shall be yours.*

*We will be bound together once more, and not for
a fleeting mortal span, but for all eternity, within the
infinite lattice of Her design.*

*The hour approaches. The strands draw taut. You are
already caught.*

Inextricably yours,
Elijah

Take **+ 1 CLUE** and the SECRET: *The Haunting of Toby Jugg.*

> Turn to **209.**

190

"So, you're passionate about the study of spiders?" Trenholm
is asking Dr Bellweather as you approach.

"Yes," she replies. "If I might be so bold, I am something of
an expert in the field of arachnology."

"Do you venture into the field much?"

"No, I'm afraid not," she says sheepishly, blushing and
looking at the floor again. "I rely on those of a rather more
adventurous bent to collect specimens and bring them back
to Miskatonic University for me."

"I brought a spider specimen back from Brazil once," says Trenholm. "I didn't mean to, of course, but it had got into a crate of pottery shards and made itself comfortable in the straw. It gave the customs inspectors a shock when the crate was opened again here in New England. Ugly critter and big, too!"

"Was it an Acanthoscurria gomesiana, by any chance?" Dr Bellweather asks him.

"No, lady, it was a tarantula."

Take the SECRET: *Bug Off.*

As Dr Bellweather lets out a sigh, it is only then that Trenholm acknowledges your presence. "And what do you do?" he asks.

Turn to **280.**

191

The library is located in the northeast corner of Harcourt House, beyond the parlor and the stairs to the second floor. The walls are lined with floor-to-ceiling bookcases of dark wood, and the two windows in the room have their curtains drawn against the night.

To your right, perusing the shelves that cover the southern wall of the library, is Professor Otto Varnum. Glancing your way, he arches an eyebrow, acknowledging your presence, and then returns to studying the spines of the books in front of him. "Can I help you?" he asks indifferently.

How will you respond?

192

You are passed on the landing by one of the housemaids. She is wearing a black dress and white apron. Her blonde hair is tied in a bun on the top of her head and covered by a mob cap. She is hurrying in the direction of Elijah Harcourt's bedroom, carrying a pile of fresh linen.

She nods to you in acknowledgment, whilst keeping her eyes cast respectfully toward the floor, before trotting on her way.

Make a fate test. Roll one die, and if you have the Weakness {CURSED} or {TROUBLED DREAMS}, deduct 1.

If the result is equal to or lower than the current **DOOM** level, turn to **108**.
If the result is greater than the current **DOOM** level, turn to **96**.

As you cross the attic space, your feet feel heavier and more sluggish with every step. But it is not physical exhaustion that is responsible – it is the struggle taking place inside your head.

Make a strength of will test. Roll one die and add your **WILLPOWER**. You may spend 1 **RESOURCE** to roll two dice and pick the highest. If you have the Weakness {**ARACHNOPHOBIA**}, deduct 1. If you have the {**ARCANE STUDIES**}, {**GUARDIAN**}, or {**MYSTIC**} Ability, add 1. If you have the Weakness {**CAUTIOUS**}, deduct 1. What's the result?

Total of 10 or more: turn to **135**.
9 or less: turn to **172**.

194

You are beginning to understand why you are here, why you came to Harcourt House on the autumnal equinox, and what it is you need to do. Take the Ability {RESOLVED}.

Take +1 SANITY for each of the items on the list you have in your possession: [DREAMER'S DIARY]; [POTTERY SHARD]; [GROTESQUE IDOL]; [THE SOMNAMBULIST'S PATH].

Roll one die. If you have the Weakness {FEAR OF INSECTS}, add 1. If you have the Weakness {TROUBLED DREAMS}, add 1. And, if you have the Weakness {ARACHNOPHOBIA}, add 2.

> If the total is equal to or less than your SANITY, turn to **69**.
>
> If the total is greater than your SANITY, turn to **26**.

"Together," you tell Trenholm, taking hold of the handle to one of the doors each. "On three. One, two, three!"

The two of you slam your weight against the doors – again and again. Finally, the wood around the lock splinters, and the doors fly open, causing you to half stumble into Harcourt's study.

However, gaining access to the room has not been without cost. You have jarred your shoulder. Take -**1 HEALTH**.

Turn to **111**.

Ignoring the attorney, you tear open the envelope, take out the letter, and begin to read.

My Dear Cora,

How curious that one so versed in webs and the patient snares of nature should stumble so clumsily when it came to weaving snares of her own. Your work with the specimens I required was commendable. In that narrow field your diligence is beyond reproach. For this, I ensured your research continued, as promised. Yet it amuses me still that you should mistake professional patronage for personal affection, and that your heart –

so earnest, so unguarded – should imagine mine could ever be swayed by such advances.

You will forgive me if I speak plainly: sentiment has no place in the matters with which I concern myself. What use have I for tender affections, when all around us greater forces stir? Yours was a fragile offering, cast into an abyss that hungers only for knowledge, sacrifice, and blood. I did not spurn you out of cruelty, but out of clarity. A surgeon does not pause his incision for the sake of the knife's feelings.

But as you so generously offered me your heart once, tonight I will receive it gladly along with the rest of you, body and soul. Comfort yourself, knowing that you are one of that number with whom I shall share the Mother's gifts.

Elijah

Take + **1 CLUE** and the SECRET: *Poison Pen Letter.*

"Now that you've read the letter, are you going to share its contents?" asks Ward pointedly.

"Oh, so now someone else has read Dr Bellweather's letter, you're quite happy to know what it was about?" challenges the explorer.

Turn to **166**.
Unless you've spotted a mysterious number hidden in the text which leads you elsewhere…

What do you have with which you could threaten the spider-thing abomination?

A [BOOK OF MATCHES] or a [LIGHTER]: turn to **208**.
A [PISTOL]: turn to **223**.
A [POTTERY SHARD]: turn to **294**.
A [GROTESQUE IDOL]: turn to **252**.
A [SYRINGE OF MORPHINE]: turn to **240**.
None of the above: turn to **281**.

You whip the pot from your pocket and remove the lid, which you notice has holes punched in it, but you will have to be quick if you are going to catch the spider before it can get away.

Make a speed test. Roll one die and add your **COMBAT**. You may spend **1 RESOURCE** to roll two dice and pick the highest. If you have the {AGILE} or {QUICK-WITTED} Ability, add 1. What's the result?

Total of 8 or more: turn to **225**.
7 or less: turn to **35**.

199

"The baleful arts. Witchcraft. Blood rites! Elijah was mad! He was willing to sacrifice a human life if that was what it took to implement what we'd pieced together from ancient texts. It was all a great experiment to him. But I wanted no part of it! And so, we went our separate ways." Take **+1 CLUE**.

Turn to **129.**

200

Wondering what sort of books a man like Elijah Harcourt might have in his personal archive, you begin to peruse the shelves. Considering how neatly the books are arranged in regimented rows, you notice several gaps, implying that someone has removed those volumes for consultation elsewhere.

In doing so, they have dropped something on the floor. Bending down you pick up the [LEATHER BOOKMARK] you find there and secret it in your pocket. Record the [LEATHER BOOKMARK] on your Character Sheet.

The books in Harcourt's collection appear to have been arranged by subject matter. The entire southern wall of the room, to the right of the door, is dedicated to books on anthropology. The corner between where the north wall and east wall meet contains books about Kingsport and the Massachusetts coast, while the shelving that abuts the fireplace in the west wall is home to great ancient leatherbound tomes, such as you might expect to see chained up in a medieval monastery somewhere in Europe, books that are little more than curling scrolls tied tight with cords of leather, and others that are black with age, bound in some cured organic material that is strangely familiar, although you cannot quite place it.

Three titles stand out in particular, one from each subject area: *Forgotten Cults of Hyperborea*; *Olde Kingsport and Its Curiosities*; and *The Somnambulist's Path*.

Which book do you want to take a closer look at?

Forgotten Cults of Hyperborea: turn to **13**.
Olde Kingsport and Its Curiosities: turn to **65**.
The Somnambulist's Path: turn to **90**.

Forgotten Cults of Hyperborea is a crumbling folio whose introduction claims it contains information gained from translating fragments of pre-human stone tablets and the lost records of the mad magus Eibon of Mhu-Thulan. It concerns the secret societies, dark heresies, and nightmare religions that proliferated within Hyperborea – that legendary, ice-haunted continent long sunk beneath the seas and preserved now only in myth.

The sects and societies listed within include the Cult of Tsathoggua, devoted to the bloated god of sloth, the snake-worshippers of Yig, the father of serpents, the frostbound sorcerers, and the children of Atlach-Nacha. It is this last one that catches your attention.

Devotees of the spider goddess seemed to believe that she dwelt in caverns deep beneath Hyperborea, weaving a colossal, never-ending web that stretched across realities with each new strand forming a bridge between worlds. Neophytes were entombed in darkness, kept alive until spiders consumed their flesh, with any survivors being considered marked by Atlach-Nacha to become her children. To the cult, the impossible web was destiny itself, and all beings were trapped within its strands. To serve the spinner in darkness was to accept and embrace one's place in the design.

Take **+1 CLUE**, gain the Ability **{STUDIOUS}**, and if you want to take the book with you, record **[FORGOTTEN CULTS OF HYPERBOREA]** on your Character Sheet.

Turn to **140**.

202

Hearing Isabel Harcourt suddenly call out your name, with the note of panic in her voice, makes you rush to her aid. But it isn't the young woman who needs help – it's Dr Harrow.

He is slumped in a chair in the parlor, his eyes closed, his cheeks flushed, sweating profusely, and his breathing has become ragged and shallow. Isabel perches on the seat next to him. His medical bag sits on the floor beside his chair.

"What happened?" you ask.

"One minute he was fine, the next he said he didn't feel very well, and in no time at all he was as you see him now," says Isabel. "If I didn't know any better, I would say he had been bitten by a venomous spider as well."

"How can you be sure he wasn't?" you challenge her.

She jumps up from her seat with a cry of alarm, desperately scouring her surroundings, searching for a spider the size of a human hand with black and red markings reminiscent of a glowering, demonic skull. At that moment, Knott the butler makes an appearance in the parlor.

"Is Dr Harrow quite well?" he asks, a tone of genuine concern in his voice.

"No, he's not," says Isabel. "He's not well at all."

"Then I shall telephone again for help," says the butler, turning on his heel and leaving as quickly as he arrived.

You, on the other hand, are fully focused on working out how you can best help Harrow.

203

Inside one of the cabinets, you can see a curved stone spike, resting on a black velvet cushion, just like the one you have in your possession. Next to it can be seen a slight hollow in the velvet, showing where its partner should lie.

However, whoever took the fang-like stone from the cabinet was careless; lying on the floor beneath the cabinet is a piece of a terracotta pot that looks like it was placed next to the cushion. The culprit's hand must have caught it as they grabbed the spike and unwittingly knocked it off the shelf. They then shut the front of the cabinet again without realizing what they had done.

Clearly once part of some larger vessel, one side of the shard – what you take to have been the outside – is painted with stick figures carrying spears attacking something. The piece of the pot showing whatever it is they are attacking has not survived, but you can see that it had lots of long legs.

As you hold it in your hands, for a moment your senses are assailed by a series of scents and sounds, as if half-remembered; the stink of a charnel chamber, the damp of subterranean tunnels, the chants of degenerate creatures that might once have been human, and a dog-like howling. Where on earth did this artifact come from?

Record the [POTTERY SHARD] on your Character Sheet.

Take +1 CLUE, +1 DOOM, and the SECRET: *Cannibalistic Humanoid Underground Dwellers.*

Intrigued by what you have discovered, what do you want to do next?

To take a look at the framed drawing, turn to **73**.
To examine the collection of photographs, turn to **224**.
To leave the museum and look elsewhere, turn to **170**.

204

Dropping to your knees, you also take out the [DREAMER'S DIARY] and lay the two books on the floor next to each other. Hurriedly flicking through the handwritten journal, you find what you are looking for – something you glimpsed the first time when you acquired the book and had a quick thumb through it. It is a page covered in the squiggles and characters of the curious language also written within *Forgotten Cults of Hyperborea*, but with English letters transposed beneath.

You may not actually understand what you are reading, but you can at least attempt to read the incantation out loud now.

Make a decoding test. Roll one die and add your **INTELLECT**. You may spend **1 CLUE** to roll two dice and pick the highest. If you have the {**ACADEMIC**} or {**STUDIOUS**} Ability, add 1. What's the result?

Total of 7 or more: turn to **165**.
6 or less: turn to **281**.

205

One of the housemaids lunges at you, her blonde hair coming loose from the bun underneath the mob cap and hanging in untidy tangles. Before she can rake your face with her fingernails, you seize her by the upper arms and hurl her against a lower roof joist. Her head strikes the beam with a sickening thud, and she collapses to the floor like a marionette with its strings cut.

Screaming incoherently, Knott barrels into you, stronger than you would have thought his age should permit, fists flailing with wild, desperate strength. You grapple, twisting to avoid his blows, your back slamming against a crossbeam as you drive a knee into his gut. He snarls, spittle flying, eyes full of madness.

Across the floorboards, Isabel grapples with the other housemaid, who shrieks and claws like a feral animal. Isabel parries with a broken chair leg she has found somewhere nearby.

"This isn't what I wanted, Uncle!" she shouts through gritted teeth, swinging hard, as the spider-thing burbles to itself. "I begged you to help me. To forgive the debts. Not... this!"

The makeshift weapon cracks against the maid's skull. The woman stumbles, dazed.

"I have danced to your tune long enough. Smiled at your guests. Laughed at your riddles. And for what? So I could be your damn Door?"

Knott lunges again, but you catch him mid-charge and slam him down. The attic fills with dust and ragged breath as you finish off the butler, just as Isabel delivers a final, splintering blow to the maid's skull with the chair leg.

Turn to **238**.

206

"Just a book I lent Elijah," replies the professor.

"What was it about?" you ask.

"Um... spider cults of South America."

"Bit left field for a historian, isn't it?" you challenge him.

"It's something of a personal interest of mine."

"And are there many?"

"I beg your pardon. Are you asking if I have many interests?"

"No, I meant are there many spider cults in South America?"

"You'd be surprised," Varnum replies. "Some of the lesser

known, more elusive ones are the Arahuka Weavers of the Amazon basin and La Red de la Araña Roja of the Paraguayan Pantanal. You'd be surprised how many groups hold spiders in high regard."

When you look at him blankly he goes on.

"There are also the Nazca Lines. A series of massive motifs created on the ground by arranging or removing natural materials like stones, gravel, or earth, but on such a scale that they can only be properly appreciated from a high vantage point – such as a mountaintop, or by airplane. The Nazca Lines were etched into the desert plains of Peru by the Nazca culture between approximately 500 BC and AD 500," he says, warming to his subject. "The book I lent Elijah goes in to far more detail, of course, and lists many more spider cults."

"And Elijah had an interest in these cults as well, did he?"

"Oh yes," Varnum replies. "For me they are an interest. For Elijah, however, they were an obsession."

Take +**1 CLUE** and the SECRET: *Bookworm*.

If you now want to ask Varnum if he has known Elijah Harcourt long, turn to **31**.

If you want to ask him what was in the letter Harcourt wrote to him, turn to **112**.

If you don't want to ask him anything else, turn to **219**.

Opening the wardrobe, you find jackets and trousers hung neatly within. But as you start to slide them aside to see what might lie at the back of the armoire, a small, dark shape suddenly flies at you from the lapel of an overcoat.

Make a reaction test. Roll one die and add your **COMBAT**. You may spend **1 RESOURCE** to roll two dice and pick the highest. If you have the {**AGILE**} Ability, add 1. What's the result?

> Total of 10 or more: turn to **267**.
> 9 or less: turn to **227**.

The sharp scratch of ignition is loud in the hush of the attic. A small flame flares into life, casting flickering light across the roof space that is reflected from thousands of tiny obsidian orbs all clinging to their thick, numerous webs.

For an instant, the thing at the center of the web recoils – not from the light itself, but from what it means. Destruction.

The flame catches a trailing strand of the great web. Silk hisses and blackens and then ignites with a whoosh of rushing air and a flash of angry orange. The fire spreads quickly, licking up the threads as if they were fuses, racing toward the heart of the web and the abomination that squats there.

The sleepers' cocoons are on fire now, but there is nothing

you can do to help them, as appalling as that knowledge is. Take -**1 SANITY**.

The creature shrieks – a sound that's part spider, part man, part something far older and ghastlier. Its limbs scrabble, skittering in panic as the flames draw ever closer, turning its sanctuary into an inferno. The blood-soaked silk burns hot and bright, and the creature's cries turn shrill, maddened, almost pleading.

Flames curl around it. Its mandibles clack furiously. Eyes bulge and burst in the heat. And then the thing that was Elijah Harcourt is engulfed.

The scream it lets out is the last true sound it will ever make, a bubbling, echoing wail. Then it is silenced – swallowed by fire and the collapsing web.

A rush of hot air blasts outward, pushing you back. Flickering embers drift like dying fireflies through the air. The impossible otherworldly portal is no more. But the nightmare is not over yet.

The web may be gone, the portal closed, but the Harcourt House of nightmares is burning.

You turn and flee the attic and then the house, taking Isabel Harcourt with you. The thick, choking fog that has clung to the house since your arrival is beginning to lift at last, thinning into shreds as if retreating from what now burns within.

The pair of you race down the drive together. Behind you, the burning house lights up the night like a colossal bonfire, casting flickering shadows across the manicured grounds and red maple trees. Smoke and ash rise into the night sky, trailing sparks.

You pass through the iron gates without looking back, not even slowing to catch your breath. The road stretches ahead, winding down toward Kingsport below, the town nestled at the foot of the cliffs.

Elijah Harcourt is dead – burned to death. So, too, are those he lured into his web, sacrificed without hesitation to feed his vile ambition and the will of his unspeakable god.

The house of spiders is burning now, its bones cracking in the heat, its secrets consumed by flame. It will not survive much longer. And if fortune allows, neither will the horrors that once nested within its walls.

Secret: *The House of the Spiders.*

Final score: 4 stars.

The End.

"Dr Harrow?"

You look up to see Harcourt's butler, and head of the household staff, climbing the staircase, with Trenholm only a few steps behind.

"At last," says an exasperated Harrow. "The professor has been stabbed. He is stable but we need to stop the bleeding. Do you have another bed available? I need to make him comfortable if we are to keep him alive."

"Of course, doctor," replies Knott.

"And where's that help you phoned for? Shouldn't they have arrived by now?"

"I agree, and I can only apologize," the butler says in a suitably apologetic tone. "A thick fog has descended outside. I can only imagine that is why they have been delayed."

"Never mind. The important thing is that we get Professor Varnum moved and keep him stable."

"Of course, Dr Harrow, but might I ask a question?"

"What?"

"Who stabbed him?"

Harrow's staring eyes look from you to Trenholm and finally back to Knott.

"I do not know. That is another matter we must contend with."

He's right, of course. The attack on Otto Varnum is indisputable proof that there is a would-be murderer hiding in plain sight in Harcourt House. Now that you know that to be the case, can you be certain that what happened to Elijah Harcourt and Cora Bellweather were unfortunate accidents, or were they, in fact, carefully orchestrated attacks planned to appear as accidents?

You know you will not be able to rest until you have gotten to the bottom of the mystery and uncovered the truth of what is going on within Harcourt House. But how do you want to proceed with your investigation?

If you want to find out what lies behind the bookcase-door, turn to **116**.

If you want to investigate Harcourt's so-called museum, turn to **142**.

If you want to go downstairs and inform the others of what has happened, turn to **233**.

210

There are maps of places from all over the world, including Indonesia, Peru, India, and the Caribbean. Photographs, drawings, and even handwritten notes have been pinned to these maps, connected to specific locations. But the one that interests you the most doesn't appear to be a map of a real place at all.

It covers the wall above the safari camp-bed and looks more like an old seafarer's map, the kind that are illuminated with images of fantastical monsters cavorting in the oceans. The longer you study it, the more convinced you are that it's entirely made up. You certainly don't recognize the arrangement of three continents and sundry islands, even though stylized drawings of the sun and moon have been included on the left and right sides respectively.

There are drawings of geographical features, such as mountains, forests and rivers, as well as cities and other landmarks. Some of them are labelled but again, they are not names of any places you know of on Earth. Take + **1 CLUE**.

The room's décor makes you think it could have easily been occupied by an explorer, but do the maps indicate places the explorer had actually been or simply locations they were hoping to visit? Or are they simply the product of a dreamer's overactive imagination?

What do you want to do now?

To take a closer look at the bed and desk, turn to **230**.
To open the cupboard and see what's inside, turn to **286**.
If you want to leave the secret map room, turn to **258**.

South Shore is Kingsport's arts and entertainment district, although you would be forgiven for mistaking it for the kind of seaside destination found in a dozen towns up and down the New England coast, chock-full of boardwalks, eateries, and other tourist traps. That said, the boardwalk has plenty to recommend it, with such standout landmarks as an electric carousel and a bustling artists' scene where one might meet the next up-and-coming legend.

It also hosts traveling carnivals, where allegedly clairvoyants practice palmistry and crystal gazing – all in return for a silver dollar, of course. The boardwalk is not as busy as it would be during the summer months, but there is still an air of fun here as the fall season closes in.

Still, with so many of those inhabiting South Shore being out-of-towners like yourself, you're not convinced that it was your best idea to come here seeking information about Harcourt House. Instead, it becomes a diverting way to spend the time until you must make your way to the mansion at the specified hour.

In that frame of mind, you decide to call on one of the visiting psychics, although you do not expect anything useful to come of the experience. Choosing a garish tent with a sandwich board outside declaring that it is the temporary residence of "Madame Zvezda, Oracle" you pull aside a purple velvet curtain and step inside.

An elderly woman, wrapped in various shawls, sits in an armchair draped with silk scarves on one side of a small, round table. She invites you to sit on the meager stool opposite her. When you have crossed her palm with the requisite piece of silver, she takes hold of your hand with her bony fingers and runs long yellow nails over the creases of your palm.

After what feels like a strangely long time for her not to speak, you prompt her with a disgruntled, "Well?"

Her beady black eyes meet your gaze, and then she speaks at last, her accent sounding like it originated from somewhere in Eastern Europe. However, you wonder if it is all part of the act.

"You have been summoned… to the house… of dreams… to the cave of nightmares."

She pauses, turning your hand over.

"Harcourt House?" you ask her, hoping for confirmation, but she waves your question away with a grunt of annoyance.

"The spinner in darkness waits… seven have been called… the ritual has already begun… but your fate…" She scowls again, re-examining your lifeline. "I cannot see!"

"That's it?" you ask her, feeling a curious combination of annoyance and uncertainty. Part of you feels like you've been ripped off, but another part of you can't help wondering whether what she has relayed to you might have a modicum of truth to it. Take **+1 CLUE**.

"Go now," she tells you. "We are done."

Seeing little point in arguing, you exit Madame Zvezda's tent and find yourself standing in front of a hall of mirrors.

If you would like to distract yourself by visiting the hall of mirrors next, turn to **247**.

If you would prefer to be on your way, turn to **150**.

You notice that the young woman's eyes are like shining black pearls, but there aren't just two of them. There are clusters of smaller orbs at the corners of each of the two eyes you would expect her to have, giving her eight in total.

All the unblinking inhuman eyes are fixed on you. Unable to tear your gaze away, you stare transfixed as the maid opens her mouth, revealing malformed mandibles rather than human teeth, and from between these shoots a jet of a sticky, silk-like substance that hits you in the face.

You close your eyes instinctively and, unable to stifle a cry of revulsion, put your fingers to your face to pull the stuff away. Only, rather than spider silk, what you pull from your face is a lace doily that has fallen from the pile of linen the housemaid is carrying.

Her features wholly human once more, she hurries down the stairs to retrieve the doily, apologizing profusely all the while, before returning to what she was doing before.

However, the curious incident leaves you feeling shaken. And knowing that it was all in your head doesn't make you feel any better. In some ways it makes it worse.

Take -**1 SANITY** and the SECRET: *Kiss of the Spider Woman.*

Turn to **202**.

As your eyes adjust to the gloom of the attic, you realize that the cluttered room is suffused with a faint purple luminescence. It puts you in mind of the glow of crystals in a huge cave, except that you are in the cramped confines of the space that exists between the joists and beams of the roof structure of Harcourt House. Your mind reels at the strange juxtaposition, how two opposites can seem true at the same time. The air is redolent with a fetidness that catches in the back of your throat.

The roof space is like another room – tall enough to stand upright in, crisscrossed by supporting ceiling beams and roof joists, and filled with the detritus of the Harcourt family over many generations. A spear of light from the hallway chandelier enters through a hole in the floor, where the silhouette of broken lathes can be seen.

As you make your tentative way into the attic, you gasp when you see what awaits you there and freeze.

Lying on the floorboards in front of you are five bundles that put you in mind of the silk-bound parcels that lie in a spider's larder. Incredibly, each is big enough to contain a human being, and you already know what the silken cocoons contain even before you identify the faces of those trapped within.

The bodies of the other guests have been wrapped in a thick web-like material, which makes it look like they are bound up in burial shrouds, leaving only their faces exposed – Dr Cora Bellweather, Professor Otto Varnum, Peregrine Ward, Luther Harrow, and even Horace Trenholm. They all look like they are asleep, their eyes closed and an expression of calm on each of their faces. However, as you watch for a moment, from

time to time you see one of them frown in consternation, as if
encountering something unpleasant in their dreams.

More sticky strands, which look like the twisted cords
of a rope, trail from each of the cocoons, winding their way
across the rough wooden floorboards of the attic deeper into
the gloom. Unable to help yourself, like a moth drawn to a
flame, you start to creep forward again, following the trail of
the silken ropes.

You can see something strung between the beams of the
attic that fills the entire space from one side to the other. It is
a colossal spider's web and squatting at the center of it is the
shadowy bulk of a gigantic spider. Your pulse quickens as your
body readies itself for flight or fight.

Despite the horrific nature of the monstrous arachnid
before you, your attention is drawn momentarily to the crystal
glow permeating the space beyond it. Looking through the
web, you can see a vast subterranean chamber, even though
you are right at the top of the house. How can that be?

The mustiness of the air in the attic is explained now, as it's
what you would expect to find underground. By the curious
purple glow, you can see vague shapes moving within the
cave. Every now and then you can identify a limb here or a
swollen abdomen there, and you realize they are spiders, too.
But considering the distances involved and the scale of the
cavernous chamber, they must be gigantic – at least as big as
the thing squatting at the center of the web in front of you.

They appear to be tending to something at the center of the
cave, something many orders of magnitude larger than the
thing here in the attic.

"What is this place?" you whisper, disturbing the eerie
quiet that reigns in this impossible space.

"You are honored, for you gaze upon the domain of
the spinner in darkness, Atlach-Nacha, deep beneath

Mount Voormithadreth," the butler suddenly replies from behind you, making you start. "You are blessed, for you will witness the apotheosis of the anointed of Atlach-Nacha."

"The anointed…?" Isabel says in a broken voice.

The thing on the web shifts, focusing your attention again on the more immediate threat to your life.

"Magnificent, isn't he?" Knott's voice said, full of awe.

You cannot help but answer his rhetorical question with a question of your own. "He? How do you know it's a…?" But the words die in your throat as the monstrosity turns its head toward you, and the strange light picks out the details of the features.

In the semi-darkness of the attic, the creature waiting within the web might have the body of a gigantic spider, but it wears the malformed face of Elijah Harcourt.

Consider the following list of items: [DREAMER'S DIARY]; [POTTERY SHARD]; [GROTESQUE IDOL]; [THE SOMNAMBULIST'S PATH].

If you are in possession of one or more of the items on the list, turn to **194**.
If you do not have any of these items, turn to **174**.

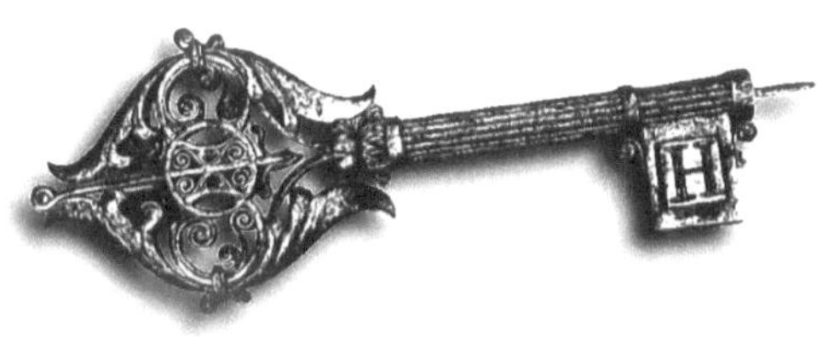

The guest bedrooms lie on the south side of Harcourt House, on the second floor.

It is eerily quiet in this part of the house, the only sound you hear being the insistent scratching of a tree branch against one of the bedroom windows somewhere nearby.

If you have a [BRASS KEY], turn to 278.
If not, turn to 249.

Despite your desire and desperation to break free, the silken bindings are already wrapped too tightly around you for you to be able to force your way out. Unable to escape, you turn your attention to your surroundings instead.

Isabel Harcourt is next to you, also half-wrapped in the thick webbing. However, lying on the floorboards in front of you are five bundles that put you in mind of the parcels that might be found in a spider's larder. Each is big enough to contain a human being, and you already know what the silken cocoons contain even though you are unable to make out the faces of those trapped within.

Sticky strands, which look like the twisted cords of a rope, trail from each of the cocoons, winding their way across the rough wooden floorboards of the attic deeper into the gloom.

Straining to see, you can just make out something strung between the beams of the attic that fills the entire space from one side to the other. It is a colossal web, and squatting at the center of it is the shadowy bulk of a monstrous spider.

Despite the horrific nature of the monstrous arachnid before you, your attention is drawn momentarily to the crystal glow permeating the space beyond it. Through the web you can see a vast subterranean chamber, even though you are right at the top of Harcourt House.

There is a mustiness to the air in the attic, as you might expect to find underground. By the curious purple glow, you can see vague shapes moving within the cave. Every now and then you can make out a limb here, or a swollen abdomen there, and you realize they are spiders, too. But considering the distances involved and the scale of the cavernous chamber, they must be gigantic – at least as big as the thing squatting at the center of the web in front of you.

"What is this place?" you whisper, disturbing the eerie quiet that reigns in this impossible space.

"You are honored, for you gaze upon the domain of the spinner in darkness, Atlach-Nach, deep beneath Mount Voormithadreth," the butler suddenly replies from behind you, making you start. "You are blessed, for you will witness the apotheosis of the anointed of Atlach-Nacha."

The thing in the web shifts, focusing your mind again on the more immediate threat to your life.

"Magnificent, isn't he?" Knott's voice comes again.

You cannot help but answer his rhetorical question with a question of your own. "He? How do you know it's a … ?" But the words die in your throat as the monstrosity turns its head toward you, and the strange light picks out the details of the features it falls upon.

In the semi-darkness of the attic, the creature that waits within the web might have the body of a gigantic spider, but it wears the malformed face of Elijah Harcourt.

The abomination climbs down from its web and crosses the dusty floorboards on eight legs that look strangely like wrongly jointed human arms but are nonetheless being used to propel it across the attic.

"Behold the Key!" you hear the butler cry out. "Flesh-bound, dream-marked, woven in shadow and chosen to fulfil this great purpose. The Key is true."

The Harcourt-spider looms over you, mouth distended, fangs twitching.

"And now the Key must turn!" comes Knott's voice again.

It is the last thing you ever hear as, with a sudden crunch of bone and a splash of warmth, your head is severed cleanly from your body between its jaws.

The End.

216

My Friend,

You will doubtless be wondering why I summoned you to Harcourt House, given that we share no prior acquaintance, while every other guest present at this exceptionel evening is numbered among my personal acquaintances. Indeed, with some of them I share a most intimate familiarity.

But despite these indisputable facts, do not mistake this for oversight, nor underestimate your significance. In fact, you have a vital part to play in tonight's proceedings. The others all have their flaws and their guilty secrets, but you alone stand unburdened – innocent of all wrongdoing, in my eyes at least – and that is enough. For it is through you that the Key shall turn, and the Door shall be opened.

Do not resist what is to come. All has been foreseen and prepared for. Simply having crossed the threshold this evening you are already enmeshed within the web of fate.

Now turn back to the section you just came from. Unless you've spotted *another* mysterious digit hidden in the letter which leads you elsewhere…

"I've been asking myself that," he says, taking another swig from his hip flask.

"And have you come to any conclusions?"

"Otto's harmless, a bumbling old dolt when it comes to everything apart from his fascination with ancient history. He wouldn't be able to look after himself if he didn't live at Miskatonic University and have other people to worry about things like what he's going to eat or wear."

"Then perhaps he was attacked because of his connection to Elijah Harcourt."

Trenholm laughs then. "His connection? I take it you haven't heard the rumors then. Not that they were really rumors –

more a statement of fact. Although there's been nothing like that between them for some time. I always wondered whether their falling out had something to do with that man... what was his name? Jugg?"

"Who's Jugg?" you ask.

"Another fool obsessed with the occult," Trenholm says. "But look, I don't know who I can trust around here – and that includes you. So, if you'll excuse me." And with that, the explorer leaves the museum. Take + **1 CLUE**.

> If this darkened room makes you feel uncomfortable and you want to leave too, turn to **170**.
> If you would rather remain and have a look around by yourself, turn to **54**.

There's nowhere to run now as the monstrous arachnids press in on you. You have no choice but to defend yourself.

You may spend **1 RESOURCE** at the start of each round to add 2 to your total for that round.

Round one: roll two dice and add your **COMBAT**. If you have the {**FIGHTER**} or {**RESOLVED**} Ability, add 1. If you have the Weakness {**ARACHNOPHOBIA**} or {**CAUTIOUS**}, deduct 1. If the total is 10 or more, you win the first round.

Round two: roll two dice and add your **COMBAT**. If you have the {**TOUGH**} Ability, add 1. If you won the first round, add 1. If you have the Weakness

{ARACHNOPHOBIA}, deduct 1. If your total is 11 or more, you win the second round.

Round three: roll two dice and add your **COMBAT**. If you have the {SURVIVOR} Ability, add 1. And if you won the second round, add 2. If you have the Weakness {ARACHNOPHOBIA}, deduct 1. If your total is 12 or more, you win the third round.

If you won all three rounds, turn to **27**.
If you won two rounds, turn to **44**.
If you lost two or more rounds, turn to **64**.

With a mumbled, "Well, if you'll excuse me," your fellow guest makes a hasty departure, leaving you alone in the library.

Wondering what sort of books a man like Elijah Harcourt might have in his personal archive, you begin to peruse the shelves. Considering how neatly the books are arranged in regimented rows, you notice several gaps, implying that someone has removed those volumes for consultation elsewhere.

In doing so, they have dropped something on the floor. Bending down you pick up the [LEATHER BOOKMARK] you find there and secret it in your pocket. Record the [LEATHER BOOKMARK] on your Character Sheet.

The books appear to have been arranged by subject matter. The entire southern wall of the room, to the right of the door, is dedicated to books on anthropology. The corner between where the north wall and east wall meet contains books about Kingsport and the Massachusetts coast, while the shelving that abuts the fireplace in the west wall is home to great ancient leatherbound tomes, such as you might expect to see chained up in a medieval monastery somewhere in Europe, books that are little more than curling scrolls tied tight with cords of leather, and others that are black with age, bound in some cured organic material that is strangely familiar, although you cannot quite place it.

Three titles stand out in particular, one from each subject area: *Forgotten Cults of Hyperborea*; *Olde Kingsport and Its Curiosities*; and *The Somnambulist's Path*.

Which book do you want to take a closer look at?

> *Forgotten Cults of Hyperborea*: turn to **13**.
> *Olde Kingsport and Its Curiosities*: turn to **65**.
> *The Somnambulist's Path*: turn to **90**.

220

"Oh, hello again," says Professor Varnum as you join him and Dr Luther at the drinks trolley. "Can I get you something? Whiskey perhaps?"

The academic gives off an air of nervousness and you can't help but wonder why.

> If you want to accept Varnum's offer of a drink, turn to **250**.
> If you would rather politely decline, turn to **280**.

Ably assisted by Isabel, the two of you take on the butler and the two housemaids. The fighting is fierce and intense – you and Isabel are driven by desperation to make it through this night alive, while Harcourt's servants are fueled by the passion of zealots. But in the end, the human desire to survive trumps the untamed insanity of Knott and the maids.

Take + **1 COMBAT** and + **1 WILLPOWER**.

Turn to **238**.

The desperate attorney shoves you out of the way, but you manage to stay on your feet. Meanwhile, Ward ducks out of the room, slamming the door behind him to hamper any potential pursuit on your part.

If you want to go after the attorney, turn to **96**.
If you would rather try to rescue whatever he was burning, turn to **241**.

You manage to get off a couple of shots, sprays of some disgusting slime flying from the holes the bullets make in the bloated body of the spider-thing. But it doesn't stand idly by and races toward you with alarming speed. You are going to have to finish this fight up close and personal.

You may spend **1 RESOURCE** at the start of each round to add 2 to your total for that round.

Round one: roll two dice and add your **COMBAT**. If you have the {**FIGHTER**} or {**RESOLVED**} Ability, add 1. If you have the Weakness {**ARACHNOPHOBIA**} or {**CAUTIOUS**}, deduct 1. If the total is 15 or more, you win the first round.

Round two: roll two dice and add your **COMBAT**. If you have the {**TOUGH**} Ability, add 1. If you won the first round, add 1. If you have the Weakness {**ARACHNOPHOBIA**}, deduct 1. If your total is 16 or more, you win the second round.

Round three: roll two dice and add your **COMBAT**. If you have the {**SURVIVOR**} Ability, add 1. And if you won the second round, add 2. If you have the Weakness {**ARACHNOPHOBIA**}, deduct 1. If your total is 17 or more, you win the third round.

> If you won two or more rounds, turn to **71**.
> If you lost two or more rounds, turn to **86**.

The photographs are a series of images of wall paintings from a cave in New Mexico. The way they have been arranged seems to tell a story, like the comics in the funny pages of a newspaper.

The story would appear to be one of devotion and self-sacrifice. A chosen group are isolated from a tribe but venerated. Then they appear to be bound in ropes and laid within a temple. In the last image, the bound chosen are shown lying beneath a huge spider-like figure.

As you decode the story hidden in the cave paintings your mind starts to play tricks on you. It must be some sort of optical illusion, but the paintings of the spiders seem to move when you glimpse them at the periphery of your vision. Yet, when you look at one directly, it is a static image captured on photographic paper.

But then, when you look away again, the spiders in the images now at the edges of your vision start to squirm.

Make a courage test. Roll one die and add your **WILLPOWER**. You may spend **1 RESOURCE** to roll two dice and pick the highest. If you have the {ARCANE STUDIES}, {MYSTIC} or {SORCERY} Ability, add 1 to the die roll. If you have the Weakness {CAUTIOUS}, deduct 1. What's the result?

> Total of 10 or more: turn to **30**.
> 9 or less: turn to **130**.

Leaping forward, you slam the pot down on top of the spider. Tipping the pot upright, you quickly pop the lid back on and screw it tight shut. Thanks to your quick thinking and swift action, you have caught the culprit – the coma-inducing spider!

Now that there is a quarter of an inch of glass between you and the arachnid, you feel much happier about examining it closely. Take +**1 SANITY**.

Holding it up in front of your face, you take in its long, multi-jointed legs, its bulbous black body and the strange, skull-like scarlet Rorschach inkblot markings, the myriad gleaming black pearls that are its eyes, and the overlarge mandibles, a droplet of clear liquid collecting at the tip of each of its needle-sharp fangs. With its legs extended, it would be as big across as your balled fist.

You still instinctively pull your head back when the spider rears up on its hind legs, thrusting its forelimbs forward in a defiant arc. Its glossy black fangs glisten beneath its raised cephalothorax, poised and ready, even though the jar's smooth surface offers it no real target. Tiny hairs on the creature's legs bristle as it vibrates slightly, a subtle warning humming through its tensed body. Although it has nowhere to run, and cannot get to you through the glass, the spider nonetheless displays the full power of its threat posture.

"Can I have a look at that?" asks Trenholm, and you hand the explorer the pot and its prisoner.

Strike the [**EMPTY GLASS JAR**] from your Character Sheet and turn to **244**.

226

You stay where you are, rooted to the spot, unable to do anything other than watch as the spiders haul Ward farther and farther upward. Upon reaching the ceiling, his body is completely swallowed by the seething mass of black-furred bodies, which then starts to move toward what you can only just see in the suffused light is a hole, the bare lathes of the ceiling's construction visible through the broken plaster.

The swarm disappears through the hole, taking the crunched, limp body of the attorney with it, until not a single spider remains anywhere within the stairwell.

You become aware of a sing-song voice then. It is Isabel and she chants a nursery rhyme.

"The itsy bitsy spider climbed up the waterspout…"

Her mind is in danger of unravelling.

Take +**1 DOOM** and the SECRET: *Itsy Bitsy Spider.*

Turn to **118.**

227

You try to jerk out of the way, but the spider lands on your chest and scuttles upward, heading for your neck. In a panic, you brush it from you, but it still manages to sink its glistening fangs into the index finger of your dominant hand. You scream and thrash your hand, flinging the creature away from you.

The spider lands on the floor and immediately darts under the bed and out of sight.

While it didn't manage to inject a full dose of venom, your finger immediately starts to sting and swell up. You don't know what kind of spider it was, but it certainly wasn't a typical house spider. You only hope it wasn't the same species as the horror that has so far put two people into a coma this evening!

Take -1 **HEALTH** and gain the Weakness {**ARACHNOPHOBIA**} if you don't have it already.

> Turn to **276.**

228

You don't remember the library having an oppressive atmosphere the last time you visited, but it does now. In fact, it makes you feel so uneasy it saps your will just to remain here. Take -1 **WILLPOWER**.

Previously, you picked out three volumes in particular, and you certainly don't feel like hanging around searching through other esoteric tomes, so which of the three books do you want to flick through now?

> *Forgotten Cults of Hyperborea*: turn to **201.**
> *Olde Kingsport and Its Curiosities*: turn to **232.**
> *The Somnambulist's Path*: turn to **180.**
> Alternatively, if you want to leave the library, turn to **170.**

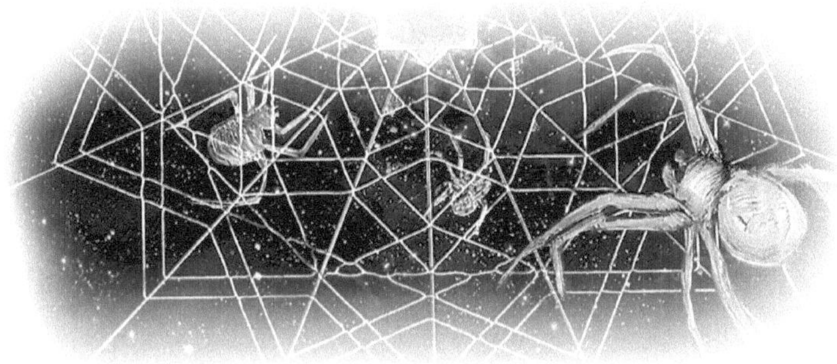

229

The webs are so thick they hang like nets over the tree. But how can this be? You do not remember seeing anything like this when you first approached Harcourt House along the drive. Could it be that you were so distracted pondering why Elijah Harcourt had summoned you to his home that you simply didn't notice?

That must be it, because the alternative is that a huge cluster of spiders have worked together to create the webs in the relatively short time since you arrived, and that seems too mind-boggling to comprehend.

As you approach the tree, the shadowy shape gains definition until it is clear you are peering at a man hanging upside down from the branches of the maple, bound up in the smothering webs.

Drawing closer, you are able to make out a beaten-up old

leather jacket. It is then that you see the satchel lying on the ground, where it has fallen at the base of the tree.

You almost dare not look at the face that is already half-covered with spider silk, but find your eyes drawn inexorably to the expression of open-mouthed horror, red-rimmed eyes staring unblinking from amidst Horace Trenholm's paralyzed features. Take - **1 SANITY**.

As you meet that glassy stare, a large black spider scuttles out of the explorer's gaping mouth, and you recoil in revulsion.

Roll one die, and if you have the Weakness **{ARACHNOPHOBIA}**, **{CURSED}**, **{FEAR OF INSECTS}**, or **{HAUNTED}**, add 1.

> If the total is equal to or less than your current **SANITY**, turn to **279**.
>
> If the total is greater than your current **SANITY**, turn to **259**.

230

You get the impression no one has slept here for some time, even though the bed has been left unmade as if its occupant only recently got up. Certainly, the presence of the hip flask would suggest someone intended to return here eventually, but the layer of dust implies they didn't.

It is then that you catch sight of something sticking out from underneath the crumpled pillow. Intrigued and unable to help yourself, you take hold of the object and pull it free.

It is a leatherbound journal, filled with slips of paper and held shut by a piece of knotted string. Pulling off the string, you open the book. Picking an excerpt at random you start to read.

It appears to be an explorer's journal, in which the unknown author has recorded their travels to all manner of exotic places. But as you read on, you realize that the places the person has visited are not in the physical world at all. They are located in a place the author calls the Dreamlands, which appears to be a parallel world of strange beauty and lurking horrors. Among its fantastical denizens, that the writer has recorded within the journal, are bestial giants, eyeless cannibalistic creatures, and a species of huge intelligent spiders that are native to a place called the Plateau of Leng.

Take **+ 1 CLUE** and the SECRET: *Living in a Dream World*. If you want to take the **[DREAMER'S DIARY]**, record it on your Character Sheet and gain **+ 1 RESOURCE**.

If you want to take a closer look at the maps and pictures on the walls, turn to **210**.
If you want to open the cupboard, turn to **286**.
If you want to leave the secret map room, turn to **258**.

231

"What are you doing?" you demand in a high, clear voice.

"Wh-what?" he stammers. "I wasn't doing anything!"

The doctor's face flushes as the hand holding the syringe starts to shake.

"Then what is the purpose of that?" you challenge, pointing at the hypodermic needle.

"I... I..." Harrow stammers again, unable to think of an excuse.

Make a deduction test. Roll one die and add your **INTELLECT**. You can spend **1 CLUE** to roll two dice and pick the highest. And if you have any of the {**DETECTIVE**}, {**GUARDIAN**}, {**STUDIOUS**} Ability, add 1 to the total.

What is the final result?

> 10 or higher: turn to **251**.
> 9 or less: turn to **271**.

232

A friendly introduction describes Kingsport as "a place of great antiquity and charm, where the sea-mist veils both past and present alike," emphasizing its "honest fisherfolk," "ancient houses," and "healthy sea air."

Replete with footnotes, *Olde Kingsport and Its Curiosities – A Visitor's Handbook to the Town by the Sea* contains a brief history of Kingsport from its origins as a Puritan settlement to a prosperous center for whaling and maritime trade as well as a whole chapter about its harbor, a list of churches and meeting-houses, and possibly more importantly, a list of inns and other drinking-houses.

Flicking on through, near the end you come to a chapter entitled "Legends of Olde Kingsport," and the book metamorphoses from a town guide to a repository of supernatural tales. Among them is a story about a phantom sailor who walks the docks at moonrise, another about dreamers who wander the mist-shrouded lanes in their sleep, never to be roused, and then the Kingsport Choir – a sound like distant chanting that is only heard on Midwinter's Eve.

Take +**1** **CLUE**, gain the Ability {**STUDIOUS**}, and if you want to take the book with you, record [**OLDE KINGSPORT AND ITS CURIOSITIES**] on your Character Sheet.

Turn to **140**.

Isabel Harcourt and Peregrine Ward are in the parlor, having an intense discussion, but break off as soon as you enter the room.

"Professor Varnum has been attacked," you tell them.

"What?" exclaims Isabel. "How?"

"He was stabbed" – you hold up the [**FOSSIL FANG**] – "with this. Dr Harrow is with him now."

"Who would do such a thing?" she asks, her voice cracking with emotion.

You hesitate before answering: "I don't know."

"Do you have any idea who it could have been?" Ward asks.

Well, do you? If you do have your suspicions regarding who could have attacked Otto Varnum, transform the letters of their surname into numbers, using the code A=1, B=2... Z=26. Add all the numbers of your suspect's last name together and then turn to the same section as the total.

A	B	C	D	E	F	G	H	I	J
1	2	3	4	5	6	7	8	9	10
K	L	M	N	O	P	Q	R	S	T
11	12	13	14	15	16	17	18	19	20
U	V	W	X	Y	Z				
21	22	23	24	25	26				

If the section makes no sense, either you have made a mistake in your addition or whoever you suspected is beyond suspicion.

> If you end up at a dead end, or you have not identified anyone who might have unleashed the spider and caused all this trouble, turn to **133**.

234

As you study the display of faience spider amulets from ancient Egypt and dreamcatchers woven by the Ojibwe people of the Great Lakes, their woven web designs inspired by the spider-woman Asibikaashi, you wonder at the dedication, and money, required to curate such a collection.

On one shelf, there is a pair of curved stone spikes lying on a black, velvet cushion. Next to the cushion is a fragment of a terracotta pot, although you cannot fathom why that should be considered worth putting on display.

What do you want to do now?

To take a look at the framed drawing, turn to **73**.

To examine the collection of photographs, turn to **224**.

To leave the museum and look elsewhere, turn to **170**.

235

"No," you tell Knott. "You stay here with Miss Harcourt. I won't be long."

Various people have either disappeared or succumbed to an unpleasant fate since you arrived at this house of spiders, including the man who summoned everyone here.

You can't shake the feeling that whatever is going on here is coming to a head. You just need more information to discover precisely what.

But where do you think you will find the final piece of the puzzle?

In the study: turn to **41**.
In the library: turn to **181**.
In the museum: turn to **142**.
In the secret room hidden behind the bookcase: turn to **74**.
In Elijah Harcourt's bedroom: turn to **62**.
In the guest bedrooms: turn to **214**.
Outside, on the grounds of the house: turn to **91**.

236

"We have a longstanding arrangement," explains Trenholm, "only it seems that Elijah has conveniently forgotten what was previously agreed. I only came here this evening to have it out with him."

At that moment, one of the housemaids slips into the room to replenish the carafe of water on the drinks trolley.

Catching sight of her, Ward arches an eyebrow. "Are you sure that was the only reason?"

"I don't know what you mean," Trenholm blusters, his own cheeks reddening now as he pointedly tries not to look at the housemaid. Take **+1 CLUE**.

"Oh, weren't we just talking about handling affairs?"

"Yes, we were, weren't we?" says the explorer, rounding on Ward again.

Turn to **266**.

237

Hurriedly finding the page about the cults of Atlach-Nacha, you come across just the thing you are looking for... you think. It certainly looks like a magical incantation, the way it is written on the page before you, but whether you can actually read it or not is another matter.

If you have the {ANCIENT LANGUAGES} Ability, turn to **165**.
If not, but you have the [DREAMER'S DIARY], turn to **204**.
If you have neither of these things, turn to **281**.

238

Harcourt's household staff lie unmoving on the rough floorboards, blood seeping from countless wounds. Crimson pools gather and mingle, dark rivers threading between limbs and broken furniture.

As you watch in frozen silence, the blood begins to move – not randomly, but with sinister purpose. Trickles wind their way toward the vast web strung across the attic. When the blood touches the strands, the silken threads darken, turning pink, then red, as though drinking it in.

A hideous, wet slurping sound cuts through the silence, stealing your attention from the dead and dying servants and dragging your gaze to the horror that squats at the heart of the web.

It takes a moment for you to realize that the spider-thing that was once Elijah Harcourt is speaking and a moment more to make sense of what it is saying.

"The Key turns… The Door opens… The anointed one arises."

Clearly, it does not matter from whence the blood has flowed, only that it has flowed. And with it, Elijah Harcourt's apotheosis is complete.

You meet the still human eyes of the spider-thing the master of Harcourt House has become and immediately wish you hadn't. Take **- 1 SANITY.**

Its mouth opens, jaws distended, lips stretching wide around chitinous mandibles, and its human vocal cords give voice to a single word: *"Hunngrrrryyy!"*

Now that you understand why you were summoned here, the role you were meant to play, what will you do?

Attack the Harcourt-spider directly: turn to **193**.
See if you have something you could use against it: turn to **197**.
Use magic: turn to **82**.
Wake the sleepers: turn to **262**.
Flee from the house: turn to **126**.
Try to escape the attic by climbing through the web: turn to **18**.

239

It's no good, you cannot find any evidence of the guilty culprit. Dejected and anxious, you head toward the study exit as you consider what to do next instead. Take - **1 INTELLECT**.

Suddenly someone cries, "Look out!" and everyone scatters.

Turning, you see a dark shape scuttling toward you on eight rippling legs. You barely have time to react before Horace Trenholm flies at the creature with what would appear to be a glass jar in one hand.

He practically throws himself at your feet and a moment later gets up again. The glass jar is still in his hand, but now with its lid screwed down tight and a hideous arachnid trapped inside it. The spider must be four inches across at least.

Its bulbous black body is covered with strange, skull-like scarlet Rorschach inkblot markings, while its eyes are myriad gleaming black pearls. Not to mention, there are the overlarge mandibles, a droplet of clear liquid collecting at the tip of each needle-like fang.

Turn to **244**.

240

Fumbling with the syringe and the vial of morphine, you fill the former with the contents of the latter, and then throw yourself at the Harcourt-horror, your improvised weapon at the ready.

Make a combat test. Roll one die and add your **COMBAT**. You may spend **1 RESOURCE** to roll two dice and pick the highest. If you have the {AGILE}, {FIGHTER}, or

{GUARDIAN} Ability, add 1. If you have the Weakness {CAUTIOUS}, deduct 1. What's the result?

> Total of 8 or more: turn to **299**.
>
> 7 or less: turn to **261**.

Hurrying over to the fireplace, you snatch the piece of burning paper from the hearth and beat it with a poker, and then your hands, to put out the flames. Although half of the paper is now no more than ashes, parts of it remain intact. It immediately becomes clear that it is a piece of writing paper, bearing Elijah Harcourt's now familiar spidery handwriting.

— ——,

__ __ ____ ____ ___ since the hubris of your embezzling came to light and I discerned the quiet siphoning of my fortunes into channels of your own contrivance. Had I chosen ____ ___ ______ ___, ______ ______ _____ __ ___ __ __ ____ _____ a curse spat in the back rooms of every firm from Boston to Providence.

Yet I stayed my hand, and in return you rendered to me a service most delicate – the preserv______ __ __ ____ __ ______, ______ ___________ __________ ____ ____ ___ _____ __ ___________. ___ ______ ___ _____ __

____ ______ _____ _________, ___ ____ _____
___ ________ ________.
____ ____ _____ ____ *delude yourself, Mr Ward, that
past obedience has purchased your release. The hour
approaches when I shall require one last service, greater
than the first and far more binding. It's nature* _ ______
____ ________ ___ _____ ______; ___ ____ _____
____ ____ ______ ___ __ _______ _______ _______
_____.

_____ _____ __ _______, ____ _____ _____
*already taken up the role that has been reserved for you,
and you will discharge it without hesitation, as before.*
    Until that hour, I remain,
    Elijah Harcourt

Take **+ 1 CLUE** and the SECRET: *Ashes to Ashes.*

> If you want to leave the study with the intent of
> catching up with Peregrine Ward, turn to **96**.
> If you would prefer to search the study to see if there
> is anything else here that might explain the attorney's
> actions, turn to **41**.

Entering the parlor, you find Horace Trenholm and Peregrine
Ward in the middle of a heated discussion.

"We should open it and read it," says the explorer, waving
an envelope in the attorney's face.

"No," says Ward firmly. "It is intended for Dr Bellweather. It is private. It should be left unopened until she is in a fit state to open and read it herself."

"If she comes out of her coma, you mean."

"Precisely."

"Which may never happen."

"So, if you are prepared to read a private letter addressed only to Cora, does that mean you would be happy to share with us what Elijah wrote to you?"

"No, I would not," is the explorer's blunt response. "But I suspect you already know what was in it, considering you're his personal attorney."

"I can assure you that I didn't even know Mr Harcourt was writing those letters, let alone what they were about."

"And yet you knew he hadn't paid me for that last lot of artifacts I brought back for him from South America, didn't you? You manage all his financial affairs as well, don't you?"

You notice a slight blush building on Ward's cheeks, but whether it is a sign of guilt, embarrassment, or anger, you cannot be sure.

Your interest has been piqued, but you're not sure whether to risk goading either the explorer or the attorney with questions of your own, or remain a silent observer to their exchange.

What do you want to do?

Pick up on Trenholm's comment about monies owed: turn to **236**.

Ask Ward if he really does manage Elijah Harcourt's affairs: turn to **266**.

Say nothing: turn to **162**.

"Just a book I lent Elijah," replies the professor.

"What was it about?" you ask.

"Um… spider cults of South America."

"Bit left field for a historian, isn't it?" you challenge him.

"It's something of a personal interest of mine."

"And are there many?"

"I beg your pardon. Are you asking if I have many interests?"

"No, I meant are there many spider cults in South America?"

"You'd be surprised," Varnum replies. "There are the secretive and elusive Arahuka Weavers of the Amazon basin and La Red de la Araña Roja of the Paraguayan Pantanal. You'd be surprised how many groups hold spiders in high regard. Then, the Nazca Lines, of course, but such a beautiful sight is not attributed to any cult."

When you look at him blankly he goes on.

"Surely, you must know of the Nazca Lines. A series of massive motifs created on the ground by arranging or removing natural materials like stones, gravel, or earth, but on such a scale that they can only be properly appreciated from a high vantage point – such as a mountaintop, or by airplane. The Nazca Lines were etched into the desert plains of Peru by the Nazca culture between approximately 500BC and AD500," he says, warming to his subject.

"And Elijah had an interest in these elusive spider cults as well, did he?"

"Oh yes," Varnum replies. "For me they are an interest. For Elijah they were an obsession."

Take +1 CLUE.

Turn to **129**.

The explorer turns the container around in his hand, closely observing its occupant.

"What kind of species is it?" you ask.

"I don't know," Trenholm replies, "I've never seen anything quite like it."

"It's certainly not your everyday house spider, is it?" says Ward, pushing his pince-nez up to the bridge of his nose, an expression of morbid fascination on his face.

"Unfortunately, the one person who could help answer that question is now lying unconscious on the floor," you point out.

"May I?" asks Harrow, holding out his hands.

"Be my guest."

As Trenholm passes the jar to the doctor, you detect a slight trembling of Harrow's hand as he takes it. If you are any judge, he must be battling his inherent arachnophobia to even touch the jar containing the spider.

Harrow places the jar on an occasional table and then starts rummaging in his doctor's bag, looking for something. He takes out a bottle with a ground glass stopper, a pair of tweezers, and a ball of cotton wool. Unstoppering the bottle, he dips the cotton wool into whatever it contains, using the tweezers. Next, he unscrews the lid of the jar and pops the damp swab inside before securing the lid again.

As he returns the items to his medical bag, the rest of you watch as the spider turns onto its back, its legs curl up underneath its body, and it silently expires.

"What did you do that for?" demands Trenholm.

"We don't want it biting anyone else, do we?" counters the doctor.

Your own morbid fascination with the creature that put two

people into a coma is growing. "Do you mind if I have a closer look?" you ask.

"Do what you want," says Harrow, tossing the jar to you. "I now have two patients to keep an eye on. We need to move Dr Bellweather upstairs to one of the guest bedrooms."

Even though it's now dead, the spider appears no less threatening, and you can almost imagine it springing back to life at any moment.

Take +1 CLUE and record the [FULL SPECIMEN JAR] on your Character Sheet.

"I need a drink," Trenholm says, making for the parlor again.

"How long until the medics get here?" Isabel asks, making her way into the front hall.

With Harcourt's guests each going their own way, what do you want to do?

Follow Horace Trenholm into the parlor: turn to **76**.

Join Isabel Harcourt in the front hall: turn to **290**.

Offer to help move Dr Bellweather upstairs: turn to **184**.

Search the study: turn to **41**.

245

You cannot leave Harcourt House while this monster exists. You have one purpose now: to thwart the ambitions of Elijah Harcourt and the entity to whom he has sworn his life, his physical being, his very soul.

Through the portal framed by the silken ropes, you can see the shadowy spider shapes moving across the cave toward the web. Whatever they are, they appear to have become aware of your presence and are rallying to the aid of their queen's chosen one.

But your primary concern is to deal with the abomination that was once Elijah Harcourt. With his niece at your side, you steel yourselves and advance together to face the nightmare in its lair.

You may spend **1 RESOURCE** at the start of each round to add 2 to your total for that round.

Round one: roll two dice and add your **COMBAT** and your **WILLPOWER**. If you have the {AGILE} or {SURVIVOR} Ability, add 1. If you have the Weakness {ARACHNOPHOBIA} or {CAUTIOUS}, deduct 1. If the total is 12 or more, you win the first round.

Round two: roll two dice and add your **COMBAT** and your **WILLPOWER**. If you have the {FIGHTER} Ability, add 1. If you have the Weakness {ARACHNOPHOBIA}, deduct 1. If you won the first round, add 2. If your total is 13 or more, you win the second round.

Round three: roll two dice and add your **COMBAT** and your **WILLPOWER**. If you have the {TOUGH} Ability, add 1. If you have the Weakness {ARACHNOPHOBIA}, deduct 1. If you won the second round, add 2. If your total is 14 or more, you win the third round.

Round four: roll two dice and add your **COMBAT** and your **WILLPOWER**. If you have the {SURVIVOR} Ability, add 1. If you have the Weakness {ARACHNOPHOBIA}, deduct 1. If you won the third round, add 3. If your total is 15 or more, you win the fourth round.

> If you won three or more rounds, turn to **71**.
> If you lost two or more rounds, turn to **86**.

You sprint after Trenholm, your heart hammering against your ribs as adrenaline floods your bloodstream. You just couldn't bear to remain inside the house a moment longer!

Take - **1 SANITY**.

Turn to **102**.

You pay your entrance fee to a stubble-faced rotund man squeezed into a tiny ticket office and step inside the hall of mirrors. The décor is as gaudy as you could hope, illuminated by lightbulbs strung on lengths of cabling. Soon, you are smiling to yourself as each mirror you pass distorts your body in new, ridiculous ways. One moment your arms and torso are elongated while your legs shrink to tiny stumps, the next your forehead bulges like a balloon, while your chest concertinas into your neck.

And then you find yourself standing in front of a mirror in which you can see no reflection at all. As you peer closer at the glass, you cannot see any smear or even the slightest settling of dust on its surface. Reaching out with a tentative hand, you go to touch the glass only for your fingers to meet no resistance at all.

You jump backward as surely as if you had received an electric shock. There is no glass in the mirror's frame, but neither can you see the back wall of the chamber through it. There is nothing but total darkness.

Only that is not entirely true. Your feet and ankles are surrounded by an eerie periwinkle colored mist that begins pouring into the hall of mirrors through the empty frame. But the darkness isn't empty. There is something there, huge and indistinct, like the black cutouts of a shadow play before the puppeteer's candles are lit.

A primal terror itches at the inside of your skull. Fear of the dark, fear of the unknown. This instinctive urge tells your body to fight or flee. It chooses the latter.

You do not stop until you are out of the hall of mirrors with your feet back on the boardwalk. You come to a sudden stop, short of breath, your pulse racing, and the vision of something monstrous emerging from the darkness beyond the glassless mirror lingers in your mind. Take -**1 SANITY** and +**1 DOOM**.

Turn to **150**.

248

"Still no sign of help?" you ask as you join Isabel in the front hall.

She shakes her head. "What are you doing here?"

"I thought you might like some company."

"That's kind of you."

But after pacing the hall for five minutes you say, "Wouldn't you be more comfortable in the parlor? Knott will answer the door when the medics arrive."

"No. I'd rather not spend any longer in there with the rest of them than absolutely necessary," she confesses.

"And why's that then?" you ask her innocently.

"Where do you want me to start?" she says, rolling her eyes and offering a wry smile. "Let's just say, being the niece of one of Kingsport's more wealthy recluses has its down sides as much as its benefits."

You smile in sympathy and then glance at the grandfather clock in the front hall. How long does it take to travel from Kingsport up the Head to Harcourt House? The cab you took couldn't have taken more than twenty minutes. But then perhaps there is an ambulance coming up the drive even now.

> If you want to open the front door and see if help is on its way, turn to **91**.
>
> If not, turn to **274**.

249

Approaching the first of the guest rooms, you carefully turn the handle, not wanting to disturb the sleep of anyone within, and peer around the jamb.

The light from the landing is enough for you to see that the bed is empty, despite the tousled sheets suggesting someone has been resting there. Perhaps you were mistaken, and this wasn't the room in which one of the victims was put.

Moving on to the second room, you throw open the door, the light from the landing spilling through to illuminate another unmade but empty bed. There is nobody here either.

Where is everyone? Where can they have gone? Take -**1 SANITY** and +**1 DOOM**.

You hurry back to the main landing and as you do so, you see that the light picks out something metallic lying on the floor. It

is a [BRASS KEY]. You pick it up and put it in your pocket.
Record the [BRASS KEY] on your Character Sheet.

> If you want to check Elijah Harcourt's room, turn to **8**.
> If you would rather go somewhere else, and you have
> a [SHIRT BUTTON], turn to **282**.
> If you would rather go somewhere else, but you do
> not have a [SHIRT BUTTON], turn to **202**.

250

Varnum unstoppers the decanter and pours you a glass while
refilling his own, sloshing whiskey over the top of the trolley
in the process, his hand is shaking so much.

"Are you all right, my old friend?" asks Dr Harrow between
lighting a cigarette and taking his first sucking draw. You
find this somewhat comical, based on Dr Harrow's gaunt
complexion.

"Nothing a glass of the old aqua vitae won't put right," says
the professor with a forced laugh. "A bit of Dutch courage.
That'll work wonders."

"And why's that?" you ask.

"Because I want to give Elijah a piece of my mind." His nostrils flare in irritation.

Having passed you your drink, Varnum clinks glasses. "Bottoms up," he declares before downing his drink in one go.

You take yours more steadily. Take +1 **RESOURCE** and the SECRET: *Dutch Courage*.

"Where are my manners?" Dr Harrow says, proffering you the crumpled packet of cigarettes. "Do you smoke?"

Turn to **280**.

251

Ah, you understand now. The secretive behavior, the shaking, the anxiety, the syringe… none of it was due to Harcourt's condition or a fear of spiders.

"That isn't for Harcourt, is it, doctor?" you say, identifying the small label on the vial. "The morphine is for you."

In that moment, Luther Harrow visibly relaxes as if you've given him the opportunity to confess. You can see the tension ease from his body. His shoulders drop, his head tilts forward, and even the tremor in his hands lessens. He carefully places the syringe back in his bag. Then, his confession pours out of him.

"A patient of mine… died. Elijah could tell something was wrong and in a moment of rash despair I confided in him. He said he would deal with the matter. That I wasn't to worry, that it wouldn't link back to me. And he did deal with it, or rather he instructed Peregrine Ward to make the problem go away. And, for some blissful time, it did. It was gone. But from that moment on, Elijah Harcourt as good as owned me. The morphine… helps me forget what I've done."

Take the SECRET: *Physician, Heal Thyself.*

"Was that what your letter was about?"

"My letter?" Harrow sounds surprised. "No. It wasn't anything like that. Here, have a look for yourself, if you want."

The doctor reaches into his bag again, but this time he takes out a crumpled envelope and holds it out to you.

"It's like the ravings of a madman, if you ask me." Take +1 **CLUE**.

> If you want to read the letter, make a note of the number **182** on your Character Sheet and then turn to **127**.
>
> If you do not want to read the letter, turn to **182** right away.

252

The transformed Harcourt starts to hiss and clack his mandibles as if in pain and retreats further into its web.

Take +1 **WILLPOWER** and the SECRET: *Caught in the Web.*

Now is your opportunity to either get out of here or press home your advantage and do away with the monstrosity altogether.

> To flee, turn to **176**.
> To finish the spider-thing, turn to **103**.

Despite all your struggling, you are unable to free yourself from the clutches of the housemaids. Either they are somehow far stronger than their slight forms would suggest, or the ordeals you have endured this night have taken a greater toll on you than you had realized.

With you and Isabel trapped in the steely grip of the two women, Knott approaches, eyes alive with ecstatic purpose.

"Behold the Key! Flesh-bound, dream-marked, woven in shadow and chosen to fulfil this great purpose. The Key is true."

Then to Isabel, restrained beside you, her eyes wide with fear.

"Behold the Door! Flesh of the anointed one, the sacrificial gate through which the supplicant will pass."

In a moment of horror, you understand the part Isabel is destined to play as the Door. She is to be a blood sacrifice!

As Knott utters the doom-laden words, you notice the unconscious Otto Varnum mouthing the words in time with the butler.

"The threshold shall open, and the anointed one will cross the bridge to commune with the web-spinning oracle, great Atlach-Nacha. Then shall the supplicant join the Mother in the great work, building the bridge between the Dreamlands and the waking world!"

He steps forward and you see now that he has a curved stone spike gripped tight in his hand. Raising it above his head he declares, "And now the Key must turn!"

Unable to fight back physically, the only weapon you have left is your tongue. But you are going to need to think quickly if you are to find the right words to stop Knott from completing the ritual.

Make a quick-thinking test. Roll one die and add your

INTELLECT. You may spend **1 CLUE** to roll two dice and pick the highest. If you have the {**ARCANE STUDIES**}, {**MYSTIC**}, {**QUICK-WITTED**}, or {**SECRET RITES**} Ability, add 1. What's the result?

> Total of 10 or more: turn to **292**.
> 9 or less: turn to **270**.

It is as if the book knows what you need it for as it falls open on a page that tells the would-be traveler to the Dreamlands of a charm to keep the Spiders of Leng – monstrous, arachnid-like inhabitants of that oneiric realm – at bay. And so, you start to read it out, exactly as it is written on the page.

> Turn to **252**.

255

Some of the shelves sag under the weight of dusty volumes with cracked spines. Others have been cleared to make room for bell jars containing preserved spider specimens, their glistening bodies suspended in yellowing fluid. And then there are those that hold all manner of arcane relics: a small idol carved from obsidian in the shape of a spider with too many eyes, a weathered silk banner embroidered with spiderwebs, and a set of brass weights depicting stylized spiders.

Elijah Harcourt appears to have something of an obsession with spiders. How ironic then that he should have been brought low by one. Or perhaps it was just always going to be a matter of time.

To look at the books arrayed on the shelves, turn to **14**.
To look at the specimens in the jars, turn to **34**.
To look at the artifacts more closely, turn to **171**.

Hurrying upstairs, you catch a glimpse of someone entering the vestibule that leads to Elijah Harcourt's museum. Following, you see the door to the museum, but also a narrow, shadowed servants' passage that leads off from it.

Hearing a stifled cry, you follow it along the passageway and find yourself at the top of a narrow flight of servants' stairs. This is how Knott and the housemaids go about their business without getting in the way of – or even being seen by – the master of the house and his guests.

But, hearing the creak of floorboards ahead, you keep going and find yourself at the foot of another narrow staircase. This one can only lead to the attic. Is Isabel Harcourt up there?

You start to climb the staircase, fearing that Isabel is in danger, but freeze when you hear the creak of floorboards again… only this time behind you. Turning, you see Isabel standing at the foot of the stairs with Knott behind her. The butler has one of her arms twisted behind her back and he is holding a knife to her throat.

Tears of terror stream down her face, but she dares not make another sound.

"After you," Knott says, pushing Isabel up the stairs in front of him and forcing you to climb all the way to the top, fearing what he might do to her if you don't obey.

As you ascend, invisible gossamer threads tickle your forehead like delicate tripwires, and you instinctively brush them away.

Turn to **213**.

257

"If you'll excuse me," Trenholm says, and with that the explorer leaves the museum.

> If this darkened room makes you feel uncomfortable and you want to leave too, turn to **170**.
> If you would rather remain and have a look around by yourself, turn to **54**.

258

Leaving the mysterious map room, you close the bookcase-door behind you, your mind full of questions. The professor is gone, the others having moved him to one of the guest bedrooms.

> If you have a [SHIRT BUTTON], turn to **282**.
> If not, but you have some [PINCE-NEZ GLASSES], turn to **10**.
> If you do not have either of these items, turn to **96**.

259

Your heart pounds and in abject terror you turn and run all the way back to the house across the lawn. Racing up the steps, you yank open the front door and throw yourself through, slamming it shut again behind you.

Take -**1 SANITY**, gain the Weakness {**ARACHNO-PHOBIA**} if you don't already have it, and make a note that you have [**DIRTY SHOES**] if you haven't already done so.

Turn to **202**.

260

Your weapon of choice is fire – a tried and trusted method for holding aggressors at bay. The flame is reflected off the myriad misshapen eyes of the monstrous things approaching you, and so you step onto the grass as you thrust the flame at one of the horrors.

As you do so, it catches a trailing gossamer thread, which immediately catches light. Despite the fog and moisture in the air, whatever the spider silk is composed of is highly combustible and the fire grows from a little flame to an inferno and spreads quickly. Soon the whole tree appears to be ablaze, with flying cinders threatening to spread it to the other maples nearby.

In response to the hungry flames, the monstrous spider-things scuttle away, vanishing into the darkness.

Knowing that the abominations are still out there in the mist and darkness, you make a hasty retreat to the house, understanding that if you are to escape this horrible house of spiders you are going to have to see this thing through to the bitter end.

Your sojourn into the grounds has left you in an agitated state. Your nerves are on edge, and your footwear is filthy. Take **-1 WILLPOWER** and record your **[DIRTY SHOES]** on your Character Sheet if you haven't done so already.

Opening the door, you let yourself back inside.

Turn to **282**.

261

The spider-thing lashes out at you with its razor-edged limbs, ripping open the flesh of your forearm and sending the syringe flying from your grasp. Take **-1 HEALTH**.

If your **HEALTH** is now zero or below, turn to **153**.
If your **HEALTH** is 1 or more, turn to **135**.

Horace Trenholm is closest to you. Grabbing him by the shoulders, the gossamer webs sticking to your hands, you shake him violently, shouting his name as you do so. Isabel does the same to Peregrine Ward. When you can't rouse Trenholm, you turn your attention to Dr Cora Bellweather.

It is as if a constellation of stars lurks in the shadowed corners of the roof space, except these stars – reflecting the eerie luminescence of the otherworldly cave rather than casting light of their own – are not constant, as movement ripples the darkness.

It takes you a moment to process what you are seeing. The angles of the attic are filled with spiders – hundreds of them – and as you struggle to wake the sleepers, they surge toward you.

If you have a [GROTESQUE IDOL] you will know how many limbs the statuette has. Multiply the number of limbs by 20 and then turn to the section with the same number as the total.

If not, turn to **275**.

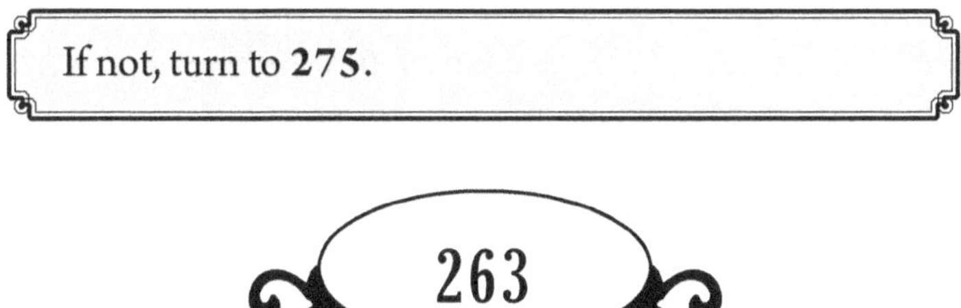

At the top of the staircase, you lean over the banister, attempting to grab Ward's hand to pull him to safety, hoping that the others will follow your lead and assist you.

You try not to scream as the first spider drops onto your shoulder, the touch of its legs feather-light but unmistakable.

Then another lands on your neck, then three more on your arms, and suddenly the swarm is upon you.

"Of course it was, it must have been," you bluster, knowing full well what you found on the floor of the study and that is now hidden inside your pocket.

Is it possible someone brought the spider into the house and somehow released it into the study with the intention of causing Elijah Harcourt harm? And if so, then who? Dr Bellweather the arachnologist? But then she would appear to have become the spider's second victim. And yet if it wasn't her, who was it? Trenholm the explorer?

"I'm just saying, you'd better watch out. We all had."

With a few simple words, Otto Varnum has you suddenly thinking that any one of those people present could be involved with a potentially murderous plot. Take the Weakness {PARANOID}.

You suddenly imagine spiders scuttling over the floor toward you and you take a step back, only for your phantom arachnids to start descending the walls on either side of the study door. You shudder and give a soft moan of revulsion. Take -**1 SANITY**.

Then someone cries, "Look out!" – you don't know who – and everyone scatters.

You are horrified to see a dark shape scuttling toward you on eight rippling legs. But you are also in possession of something that could be used to trap it.

> If you want to try to catch the spider, turn to **198**.
> If you would rather keep out of its way, turn to **284**.

265

You kick and struggle for all you are worth, and steadily the bonds of silk start to give until you tear free of them. You glance behind you, half-expecting another attack, but whatever was wrapping you in the webbing has retreated into the shadows.

Isabel Harcourt is next to you, also half-wrapped in the thick webbing. You help her tear herself free of the sticky substance. Turning your attention back to what is in front of you, you cannot help but let out a gasp of shock when you see what is lying on the floorboards of the attic.

There are five bundles that put you in mind of the silk-bound parcels that lie in a spider's larder. Incredibly, each is big enough to contain a human being, and you already know what the silken cocoons hold even before you can make out the faces of those trapped within.

The other guests have been wrapped in the same thick web-like material that you were being covered with, which makes it look like they are swathed in burial shrouds that leave only their faces exposed – Dr Cora Bellweather, Professor Otto Varnum, Peregrine Ward, Luther Harrow, and even Horace

Trenholm. They look like they are asleep, their eyes closed and an expression of calm on all their faces. However, as you watch for a moment, from time to time you see one of them frown in consternation, as if encountering something unpleasant in their dreams.

More sticky strands, which look like the twisted cords of a rope, trail from each of the cocoons, winding their way across the rough wooden floorboards of the attic deeper into the gloom. Unable to help yourself, like a moth drawn to a flame, you start to creep forward again, following the trail of the silken ropes.

You can see something strung between the beams of the attic that fills the entire space from one side to the other. It is a vast spider's web and squatting at the center of it is the shadowy bulk of a colossal spider. Your pulse quickens as your body readies itself for flight or fight.

Despite the horrific nature of the monstrous arachnid before you, your attention is drawn momentarily to the crystal glow permeating the space beyond it. Looking through the web, beyond it you can see a vast subterranean chamber, even though you are right at the top of the house.

There is a mustiness to the air in the attic, as you might expect to find underground. By the curious purple glow, you can see vague shapes moving within the cave. Every now and then you are able to make out a limb here, or a swollen abdomen there, and you realize they are spiders, too. But considering the distances involved and the scale of the cavernous chamber, they must be gigantic – at least as big as the thing squatting at the center of the web in front of you.

They appear to be tending to something at the center of the cave, something many orders of magnitude larger than the monstrosity in the attic. Something that shakes your sanity and threatens to shatter it.

265

"What is this place?" you whisper, disturbing the eerie quiet that reigns in this impossible space.

"You are honored, for you gaze upon the domain of the spinner in darkness, Atlach-Nach, deep beneath Mount Voormithadreth," the butler suddenly replies from behind you, making you start. "You are blessed, for you will witness the apotheosis of the anointed of Atlach-Nacha."

"The anointed … ?" Isabel says in a broken voice.

The thing in the web shifts, focusing your mind again on the more immediate threat to your life.

"Magnificent, isn't he?" Knott's voice comes again.

You cannot help but answer his rhetorical question with a question of your own: "He? How do you know it's a … ?" But the words die in your throat as the monstrosity turns its head toward you, and the strange light picks out the details of the features it falls upon.

In the semi-darkness of the attic, the creature that waits within the web might have the body of a gigantic spider, but it wears the malformed face of Elijah Harcourt.

Consider the following list of items: [DREAMER'S DIARY]; [POTTERY SHARD]; [GROTESQUE IDOL]; [THE SOMNAMBULIST'S PATH].

If you are in possession of one or more of the items on the list, turn to **194**.

If you do not have any of these items, turn to **174**.

"As Mr Harcourt's attorney, it is only to be expected that I would handle his affairs," is Ward's measured response.

"And not just the financial ones," says Trenholm.

The attorney fixes the explorer with a steely gaze through his pince-nez glasses. "What are you implying? I would recommend you choose your next words very carefully."

"Perhaps we should ask Luther Harrow."

Peregrine Ward looks like he is about to rise to Trenholm's verbal bait but then thinks better of it. Take **+1 CLUE**.

Turn to **162**.

Reacting on instinct, you bat the large spider away and it lands on the floor. You spin around, not daring to take your eyes off the thing as it scuttles across the room. You fear it might try to jump on you again, but instead, it disappears under the bed.

You're not sure what species it is, but it certainly isn't your typical house spider.

If you have the Weakness **{ARACHNOPHOBIA}**, take **-1 WILLPOWER**.

If you want to look under the bed to see what the spider is doing now, turn to **4**.
If not, turn to **276**.

268

"Oh yes," replies the academic, "years."

"So, you're close," you add.

"We were once, but not now." A wistful look enters his eye.

"Can I ask why?"

The professor hesitates before replying. "We had a difference of opinion."

"What sort of difference of opinion?"

Varnum gives a heartfelt sigh. "Elijah wanted to take our mutual studies to the next stage, and I didn't."

"What do you mean by 'the next stage'?" you ask.

"To move from the hypothetical to the practical. He wanted to take the step from academic study to actual reenactment."

"And you disagreed."

"I most certainly did. While I may have an interest in the occult, I am not interested in practicing black magic."

Take + **1 CLUE**.

If you want to ask him what he means by "black magic," turn to **199**.

If you want to ask the professor what he's looking for, turn to **243**.

If you want to ask what was in his letter from Elijah, turn to **112**.

If you are done interrogating the man, turn to **219**.

"We should stay together," you tell the other two.

"That's a good point," Isabel agrees. She's trembling, the events of the night clearly taking a toll on her.

"This way," says Knott, leading you toward the servants' passage and the kitchens.

But before you reach the kitchens, you find yourselves at the foot of a set of narrow servants' stairs that allows the servants to go about their business without getting in the way of – or even being seen by – the master of the house and any guests he might be entertaining.

"Up here," the butler says, setting off up the stairs.

You and Isabel obediently follow.

Upon reaching the second floor, Knott turns right, leading you to another flight of narrow, unadorned stairs. "After you," he says politely, ushering you and Isabel forward.

As you start to climb the stairs, as invisible gossamer threads catch against your forehead like delicate tripwires, and you instinctively brush them away.

Reaching the top, you find yourself embraced by the darkness of what must surely be the attic of Harcourt House.

Turn to **213**.

270

Overwhelmed by the situation you now find yourself in, you cannot think of anything to say that would stop the butler from completing the ritual he has embarked upon.

Knott brings the spike down sharply, putting all his strength behind the stroke and plunging the fossil fang into your chest. You cry out in shock and pain as the sacrificial weapon smashes through your ribcage and punctures your heart.

Knott pulls the fossil fang free again and blood gushes from the wound. Your body sags, but before you black out you hear the butler speak again. "And the Door opens!"

The last thing you hear before oblivion takes you is Isabel Harcourt's own cry of terror and agony as she is sacrificed so that her uncle might have his dream come true and ascend to join his blasphemous god.

The End.

271

You're not sure what Dr Harrow is up to, but whatever it is, you do not believe it to be above board. But how do you want to react to this unsettling discovery?

> If you want to threaten to expose the doctor by revealing the truth to the others, turn to **291**.
> If you believe that either yourself or Elijah Harcourt are in danger from the man and want to act quickly to stop him from causing anyone any harm, turn to **21**.

272

The diminutive Knott appears at the door to the study. "Dr Harrow has completed his examination of Mr Harcourt and has asked if everyone can gather in the parlor," he says, his voice an expressionless monotone, and then he disappears again.

"Any sign of the culprit?" you ask the zoologist as you make for the door.

"Not yet," she says without looking up. "You go ahead. I'll keep looking."

You arrive in the parlor to hear Isabel Harcourt ask, "How is my uncle?"

"Still unconscious," replies Doctor Harrow, "but the household staff are taking turns to check in on him, as will I."

"And was his condition caused by a spider bite?" asks Peregrine Ward.

"Of that I am certain," says the doctor.

At that moment, Knott the butler appears at Dr Harrow's shoulder.

"Is medical assistance on the way?" the doctor asks.

"Yes," replies Knott, "medical assistance is on its way."

"How long until it's here?" Professor Varnum asks.

"Within the hour," says Knott.

"So, what are we supposed to do while we wait?" asks Trenholm.

"We could find out why my uncle summoned us all here," Isabel says, holding up the wad of sealed envelopes that were on the desk in Harcourt's study. "I mean, I would imagine that's what these contain. An answer."

"About why he gathered everyone here, on this night in particular?" you ask.

"If we open our letters, maybe we'll find out."

"We might as well," sighs Ward.

"Let me, Miss Harcourt," says Knott, and she automatically hands them over.

The butler distributes the letters, reading out each recipient's name in turn. When he reads out your name, you take the envelope and retreat to a corner of the room.

The parlor goes quiet as everyone present reads their letter from Elijah Harcourt. You cannot help noticing how the others are shooting each other suspicious glances, and you get the feeling, not for the first time this evening, that they all knew each other prior to gathering at the house this night.

> You may read your letter at any time. Whenever you
> wish to do so, you should make a note of the section
> you are on at the time and then turn to **216**.
> However, now turn to **20**.

273

"You know I manage Mr Harcourt's affairs," Ward says.

"But you didn't have a hand in arranging this evening's soiree?" challenges Trenholm.

"Like the rest of you, Mr Harcourt asked me to attend him at home this evening. He didn't tell me why."

You get the feeling you aren't going to learn anything else by listening to the explorer and the attorney bicker, but you might if you explored Harcourt House by yourself while everyone else appears to be distracted.

To search the study, turn to **41**.
To look for the library, turn to **181**.
To go upstairs to check on Elijah Harcourt, turn to **62**.
To step outside, turn to **91**.

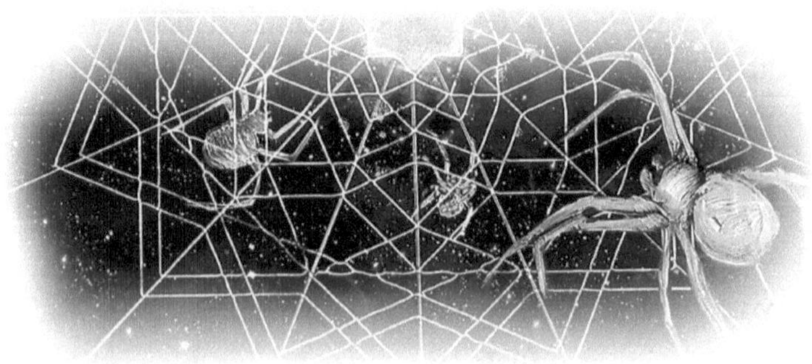

You can't bear to stand here doing nothing a moment longer. There's something going on in Harcourt House and you are determined to discover what it is.

Making your excuses and offering Isabel your apologies, you decide where to go next.

> To return to the study, turn to **41**.
> To go upstairs to check on Elijah Harcourt, turn to **62**.
> To wait in the parlor, turn to **242**.

The spiders swarm toward you – more and more of the terrifying creatures emerging from every nook and cranny, scampering over the immobile sleepers – until they are scurrying up your legs.

Having no other choice, you start to beat them off with your bare hands.

Make a struggle test. Roll one die and add your **COMBAT**. You may spend **1 RESOURCE** to roll two dice and pick the highest. If you have the {**SURVIVOR**} Ability, or the Weakness {**ARACHNOPHOBIA**} or {**CAUTIOUS**}, add 1. What's the result?

> Total of 8 or more: turn to **24**.
> 7 or less: turn to **45**.

276

The sounds of a loud commotion reach you from somewhere else within Harcourt House.

> If you have the [PINCE-NEZ GLASSES],
> turn to **48.**
> If not, turn to **170.**

277

You cannot bear to remain in the parlor while Peregrine Ward is effectively casting you as the guilty party in the night's proceedings. You step out into the hallway, taking several measured steps toward the staircase, to calm yourself down before considering what to do next.

However, while you are standing there at the foot of the stairs, Ward hurries out of the parlor, crosses the front hall, and enters Elijah Harcourt's study. What is he up to?

> To follow Peregrine Ward into the study, turn to **17.**
> To visit the library, turn to **181.**
> To explore the museum, turn to **142.**
> To enter the recently revealed secret room behind the bookcase, turn to **74.**
> To check on Elijah Harcourt in his bedroom, turn to **62.**
> Alternatively, if you want to leave the house and look outside, turn to **91.**

Nothing has changed since the last time you checked the guest rooms. They are still empty, Dr Cora Bellweather and Professor Otto Varnum are still missing. Take + **1 DOOM**.

> If you want to check Elijah Harcourt's room, turn to **8**.
>
> If you would rather go somewhere else, and you have a [**SHIRT BUTTON**], turn to **282**.
>
> If you would rather go somewhere else, but you do not have a [**SHIRT BUTTON**], turn to **202**.

Trenholm must have dropped his satchel when he ended up upside down in the tree… but you don't want to think about how that happened. You could take the scuffed leather bag, but you will have to crawl under the web-smothered maple to do so.

> If you want to crawl under the tree to take the satchel, turn to **298**.
>
> If you would rather return to the house before you run into whatever trapped Trenholm in the tree, turn to **87**.

You open your mouth to speak, but before you can answer, a bell rings somewhere within the house. Knott the butler interrupts the conversation. "Mr Harcourt is ready for you now. If you would like to make your way to his study…" He indicates a set of closed double doors across the hall from the parlor.

The seven of you dutifully troop across the hall, led by Horace Trenholm. Rattling the handle of one of the doors, he announces, "It won't open. It's locked."

"Excuse me, sir," says Knott, remaining impassively calm, "let me try."

He confidently tries the other door himself, and his unflappable façade slips for the first time. "You are right, sir." He taps on the door with a knuckle. "Mr Harcourt, sir? Are you all right?"

There comes no reply.

"Is there another way in and out of the study?" you ask, stepping forward.

"There are the windows from the garden," says Knott, a look of bewilderment on his face, "but Mr Harcourt always keeps them locked."

"Harcourt!" barks Trenholm. "What are you playing at? Let us in!"

If you have the {ROGUE} Ability or the Weakness {CRIMINAL}, turn to **295**.
If not, turn to **195**.

281

With startling speed, which is belied by its size, the Harcourt-spider leaps across the attic and strikes you with one of its razor-like limbs, breaking your concentration as well as tearing your flesh. Take -**1 HEALTH**.

> If your **HEALTH** is now zero or below, turn to **153**.
> If your **HEALTH** is 1 or more, turn to **135**.

282

A shrill scream echoes throughout the house.

Isabel Harcourt! What could have happened to her?

Following the source of the sound, your heart racing, you make your way to the central staircase. But did the scream come from the first floor or the second floor?

> If you want to look for Isabel on the first floor, turn to **296**.
> If you want to look for Isabel on the second floor, turn to **256**.

You slowly come to awareness and find yourself in an upright position, swaddled in darkness. You wonder how long you have been unconscious. Blinking yourself back to full alertness, you try to ignore the headache throbbing behind your temples as your eyes adjust to the gloom.

With beams and joists solidifying from the murky shadows around you, you work out that you are more than likely in the attic of Harcourt House. Not only that, but you are also immobile. Whoever ambushed you and brought you here has wrapped you in something that keeps your arms pinned to your sides. Take the Secret: Ambushed.

In fact, someone standing behind you is still wrapping you up, but with what?

The attic is like any other room – tall enough to stand fully upright, crisscrossed by supporting ceiling beams and roof joists, and filled with the detritus of the Harcourt family over many generations. A spear of light from the hallway chandelier enters through a hole in the floor, where the silhouette of broken lathes can be seen.

The space is also suffused with a faint purple luminescence. Looking down, it is by this eerie light that you deduce that you are being bound with spider silk!

Your heart quickening, on the verge of panicking, you writhe and fight back, attempting to free yourself from the binding silk.

Roll one die and add your **COMBAT** and your **HEALTH**. If you have the {**AGILE**}; {**FIGHTER**}; {**SURVIVOR**}; or {**TOUGH**} Ability, add 1.

What's the result?

Total of 12 or more: turn to **265**.
11 or less: turn to **215**.

You back away from the spider, determined not to let it touch you, and then, as it continues to draw closer, sidestep out of its way.

Suddenly, Horace Trenholm comes flying out of the study with what would appear to be an empty glass jar in one hand. He practically throws himself on the spider – which must be four inches across at least – and a moment later gets to his feet again. The glass jar is still in his hand, but now with its lid screwed down tight and a hideous arachnid trapped inside.

Its bulbous black body is covered with strange, skull-like scarlet Rorschach inkblot markings, while its eyes are myriad gleaming black pearls. And then there are the overlarge mandibles, a droplet of clear liquid collecting at the tip of each needle-like fang.

The rugged explorer is certainly much braver than you. Take -**1 WILLPOWER** and the Weakness **{CAUTIOUS}**.

Turn to **244**.

285

You wait respectfully until Dr Harrow and Horace Trenholm have moved the unconscious Elijah Harcourt from the room. But before you can take a good look at the desk, Harcourt's niece, Isabel, picks up the pile of letters from the desk, saying, "I'll take those," and promptly exits the study, making her way to the parlor.

If you want to follow her, turn to **173**.
If you want to remain where you are, turn to **55**.

286

Opening the cupboard, a musty smell hits your nostrils, and you immediately jump backward in shock when you realize what is hidden within.

The cupboard is, in fact, a closet, its dusty corners thick with cobwebs, as is the body propped in one corner. As far as you can tell, it is that of a man, although it is now little more than an emaciated skeleton covered in papery gray skin as dry as parchment, and still dressed in the clothes the man died in.

The body has mummified inside the airless closet, and the

drying process has exposed long yellow teeth as the lips and gums have withdrawn. Where the man's eyes were are now dust-filled sockets.

As you stare at the corpse in horror, a large spider scuttles over one shoulder and across the collapsed chest. Then a second runs over the near hairless pate, taking shelter within an eye socket.

The body suddenly starts to shudder! You can see something moving under the mummy's ragged clothes. But then that movement seems to somehow transfer to the limbs of the corpse, and suddenly the desiccated remains of the long-dead man lurch clear of the closet, arms flailing before it. The fact that it doesn't make a sound, other than a dry rustling as it moves, is almost the most disturbing thing of all. Take -**2 SANITY**.

As the corpse stumbles toward you, shedding spiders from within the folds of its clothes as it does so, you are forced to defend yourself.

You may spend **1 RESOURCE** at the start of each round to add 2 to your total for that round – if you have the **RESOURCE** to spend, that is.

Round one: roll two dice and add your **COMBAT** and your **WILLPOWER**. If you have the {**SURVIVOR**} Ability, add 1. If you have the Weakness {**ARACHNOPHOBIA**} or {**CAUTIOUS**}, deduct 1. If the total is 14 or more, you win the first round.

Round two: roll two dice and add your **COMBAT** and your **WILLPOWER**. If you have the {**TOUGH**} Ability, add 1. If you have the Weakness {**ARACHNOPHOBIA**}, deduct 1. If you won the first round, add 2. If your total is 15 or more, you win the second round.

If you won the second round, turn to **59**.
If you lost the second round, turn to **141**.

Hurrying across the landing, you enter the vestibule and see that as well as the door to the museum leading off it, there is also a narrow, shadowed servants' passage. This must be where the figure went.

Heading along the passageway you find yourself at the top of a narrow flight of servants' stairs. This is how Knott and the housemaids go about their business without getting in the way of – or even being seen by – the master of the house and his guests.

But, hearing the creak of floorboards ahead, you keep up the pursuit and find yourself at the foot of another narrow staircase. This one can only lead to the attic.

As you are wondering if that is where the mysterious figure you are following has gone, you hear the creak of floorboards again, only this time behind you. You start to turn but something heavy strikes you across the middle of your shoulder blades, then another on your head, the force of the blow knocking you unconscious. Take - **1 HEALTH**.

Turn to **283**.

You find Isabel and Dr Harrow comforting each other at the foot of the stairs. When you re-enter the house, they both turn to look at you, their eyes wide with the horrors they have witnessed.

"They took him!" Isabel says in a voice of quiet disbelief, tears of terror streaming down her face, her whole body shaking, clearly in a state of shock. "They just took him!"

"Took him where?"

Dr Harrow says nothing but merely points at the ceiling high above.

The first thing you notice is that you can see bare plaster. Not a single spider remains.

The second thing you notice is that there is a hole, where the bare lathes of the ceiling's construction can be seen.

"We have to get out of here," says Isabel, her voice possessed of a fearful tremor. "Do what Horace did and run and never look back!"

"No," says Dr Harrow, finding his own voice at last. He is evidently trying hard to remain calm, although his hands are possessed of an unmistakable palsy. "We have to stick together."

He gives you and Isabel a pleading look. Then an idea strikes him. "We should call for help. Yes, that's what we should do. Call for help."

There is another option. You could try to find out where the spiders have taken Ward.

If you want to go with Dr Harrow's plan, turn to **152.**

If you want to suggest looking for Ward, turn to **134.**

If you want to do something else, turn to **175.**

The study feels dark and oppressive, and you keep thinking you can see something moving at the periphery of your vision. However, when you turn your head to see what it is, there is nothing there, and you find the scuttling shadows have uncannily shifted to haunt the corners of your eyes again, remaining always just out of sight. Take -**1 SANITY**.

If you have a [SHIRT BUTTON], turn to **282**.
If not, but you have some [PINCE-NEZ GLASSES], turn to **10**.
If not, but you have a [FOSSIL FANG], turn to **96**.
If not, but you have a [FULL SPECIMEN JAR], turn to **162**.
If you do not have any of the above items, turn to **272**.

"Within the hour. That was what Knott said," you say, answering her unaddressed question. "But that must have been half an hour ago now."

"I'll wait for them here anyway," she responds.

"Wouldn't you be more comfortable in the parlor? Knott will answer the door when they arrive."

"No. I'd rather not spend any more time in there with the rest of them than absolutely necessary," she confesses.

"And why's that then?" you ask her, curious.

"Where do you want me to start?" She rolls her eyes and offers a wry smile.

You look at the grandfather clock in the front hall. How long does it really take to travel from Kingsport up the Head to Harcourt House? Is there even a hospital in Kingsport? You aren't sure, but you do know the cab you took couldn't have taken more than twenty minutes. But then perhaps there is an ambulance coming up the drive even now.

> If you want to open the front door and see if help is on its way, turn to **91**.
>
> If not, turn to **274**.

291

"I'm going to expose you!" you tell the doctor, backing toward the door. "I don't know what you're doing here, or what part you had to play in Mr Harcourt being in this state, but I'm sure that with Mr Ward's help we'll be able to get to the bottom of the matter."

"Ward? Ha!" Harrow gives a harsh laugh. "You clearly don't know who you're dealing with. He's not the upstanding legal professional you believe him to be. Yes, I have issues around opioids, but his record is hardly blemish free."

"What do you mean?" you ask, suddenly wrongfooted.

"I mean Harcourt has Ward in one pocket and me in the other. He owns us both!"

You don't like what you are hearing, partly because it makes you doubt how reliable a judge you are of someone's character.

Secret: *A Law Unto Himself.*

Turn to **182**.

292

"I am the Key!" you declare with an almost evangelical zeal. "I am indeed blessed to have been chosen to open the Door for the anointed one."

Knott looks slightly taken aback. But having wrongfooted him, holding out your hand to him you say, "Let me strike the sacrificial blow."

For a moment it looks like Knott is going to hand you the stone spike. The housemaid holding you relaxes her grip slightly. But it is enough.

Taking hold of the [FOSSIL FANG] you are carrying, you pull free of the housemaid and plunge the stone spike's sharp tip into the butler's chest.

Knott staggers backward, gasping in shock, his eyes wide as dark blood starts to pump from the wound, and then sits down hard on the floor of the attic. Losing all semblance of control, the housemaids give voice to terrible shrieks and go for you. They look like they are ready to rend you limb from limb with their bare hands. And suddenly you are once again in danger of losing your life!

You may spend **1 RESOURCE** at the start of each round to add 2 to your total for that round.

Round one: roll two dice and add your **COMBAT** and your **WILLPOWER**. If you have the {**FIGHTER**} Ability, add 1. If you have the Weakness {**CAUTIOUS**}, deduct 1. If the total is 14 or more, you win the first round.

Round two: roll two dice and add your **COMBAT** and your **WILLPOWER**. If you have the {**TOUGH**} Ability, add 1. If you won the first round, add 2. If your total is 15 or more, you win the second round.

If you won the second round, turn to **238**.
If you lost the second round, turn to **84**.

293

As you are moving the books around on the shelves to get a better look at them, something falls out of one of the volumes. Bending down, you see that it is a [LETTER OPENER] that was probably being used as an improvised bookmark.

You pick it up and put it in your pocket. Record the [LETTER OPENER] on your Character Sheet, take +**1 RESOURCE**, and the SECRET: *Hidden One*.

Turn to **289**.

You hold the piece of pottery, with its strange stick figures, out toward the monstrosity.

The transformed Harcourt starts to hiss and clack its mandibles and lashes out at you with one claw-tipped humanoid-arachnid limb. However, you could almost believe the monster is scared! Take ‑1 **HEALTH**, +1 **WILLPOWER**, and the Secret: *The Ritual of Chűd.*

Now is your opportunity to either get out of here or press home your advantage and do away with the monstrosity altogether.

> To flee, turn to **176**.
> To finish the spider-thing, turn to **103**.

Your life experiences up to this point have meant you have acquired certain skills, one of which proves useful to you now. Slipping your lock picking tools from a pocket, you set to work and in no time at all you hear the familiar click of a lock opening.

Turning the handle, you push open the door to Elijah Harcourt's study.

Take the Secret: *No Lock Shall Hold Me.*

> Turn to **111**.

296

You head farther along the passageway toward the kitchens. You've not been in this part of Harcourt House yet. You pass a set of narrow servants' stairs that allows the servants to go about their business without getting in the way of – or even being seen by – the master of the house and any guests he might be entertaining.

Reaching the kitchens you surprise the two housemaids who are working there.

"I hope I'm not interrupting anything," you say, stepping into the room. One of the young women opens her mouth, as if about to speak.

"Do you happen to know where–"

Before you can finish your question, you see her gaze shift from you to something behind you. You fall silent.

Feeling the hackles rise on the back of your neck, you start to turn as something heavy strikes you in the middle of your shoulder blades and then cracks you over the head. The force of the blow knocks you unconscious. Take **-1 HEALTH**.

Turn to **283**.

297

Doing your best to shut out every unsettling sight, sound and smell that confronts you in the attic, you turn your focus inward to bring your magical gift to the forefront.

Make a sorcery test. Roll one die and add your **WILLPOWER**. You may spend **1 RESOURCE** to roll two dice and pick the highest. If you have the Weakness {**ARACHNOPHOBIA**} or {**TROUBLED DREAMS**}, deduct 1. If you have the {**MYSTIC**} Ability, add 1. What's the result?

Total of 10 or more: turn to **252**.
9 or less: turn to **281**.

Your breath caught in your throat, you duck under the tree, grab the satchel by its strap, and yank it free. But as you do so, a large spider scuttles over the surface of the bag, making you scream and startle back. It charges for your hand, as if intending to bite you. Shaking the bag violently, you send the creepy-crawly tumbling to the ground, where it disappears into the grass.

Record the [SATCHEL] on your Character Sheet and take -**1 SANITY**.

Opening it, you find Harcourt's battered stainless steel hip flask, the letter Harcourt wrote to him, and a soapstone sculpture, only a little larger than your hand, that puts you in mind of a death goddess. The demonic deity is depicted as having six arms, giving her a total of eight limbs, and her otherwise human face has been pushed out of shape by the addition of a great pair of fangs. The spider-woman's eyes are glittering, cut rubies.

If you want to take either the [BATTERED HIP FLASK] or the [GROTESQUE IDOL], record them on your Character Sheet and gain +**1 RESOURCE** for each one you take.

You may read Harcourt's letter to Horace Trenholm at any time. Whenever you wish to do so, make a note of the section you are on at the time and then turn to **117**.

Now that you have the [SATCHEL] you do not feel the need to remain outside in the misty gardens any longer. Turn to **87**.

299

You manage to evade the spider-thing's flailing limbs and plunge the syringe into the bloated mass of its body. The abomination shudders and lets out a mewling cry that is like nothing you have ever heard before.

You are determined to finish what you have started, and with Isabel Harcourt at your side, the two of you prepare to battle the monster in its lair.

You may spend **1 RESOURCE** at the start of each round to add 2 to your total for that round.

Round one: roll two dice and add your **COMBAT** and your **WILLPOWER**. If you have the {AGILE}, {RESOLVED} or {SURVIVOR} Ability, add 1. If you have the Weakness {CAUTIOUS}, deduct 1. If the total is 14 or more, you win the first round.

Round two: roll two dice and add your **COMBAT** and your **WILLPOWER**. If you have the {FIGHTER} or {TOUGH} Ability, add 1. If you won the first round, add 2. If your total is 15 or more, you win the second round.

> If you won the second round, turn to **71**.
> If you lost the second round, turn to **153**.

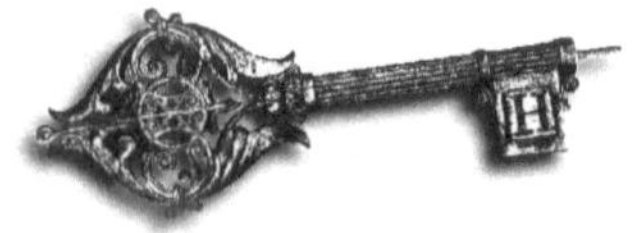

As you intone the final words of the spell, the strands of the great web begin to sag and fray. One by one, they unravel until at last the entire structure comes apart. With each thread that falls, the view of the cave beyond flickers and fades. Piece by piece, that alien subterranean realm vanishes, replaced by the cluttered beams and shadows of the attic.

The thing that was previously Elijah Harcourt lets out a terrible, keening wail as the portal falters. When the last strand falls and the gateway fully collapses, he vanishes with it – either drawn back into the abyssal domain of Atlach-Nacha or swallowed whole by the encroaching darkness splitting this world from the Dreamlands. You can't be sure which.

With Harcourt gone and the web-portal sealed, the silence returns. The strange arachnid entities that dwell here slip once more into the shadowed corners. You turn your attention to the sleepers.

They lie perfectly still in the preternatural gloom, eyes closed as if in peaceful slumber. For a moment, you tell yourself they're only unconscious – stunned, perhaps, by the ritual.

Heart still pounding from the collapse of the portal, you crouch beside Otto Varnum. Coils of dread tighten in your gut. The professor's chest is still. Tearing free the webbing from around his neck, warily you put two fingers to his throat, but there is no pulse.

You turn your attention to Cora Bellweather, daring to hope for a moment that the professor is only dead because he was stabbed with the fossilized spider fang. That hope is soon dashed when you find her in the same state. No breath. No pulse.

A strange stillness permeates the room now, as if the air itself is holding its breath.

They're dead – all five of them.

A sour wave of nausea hits you. You stagger back, hands trembling. Did the spell do this? Did Harcourt? Or was this the price of closing the portal to the realm of Atlach-Nacha?

You hear a faint rustle in the rafters above – the soft chitter of chitinous limbs retreating into the darkness – and for a moment you wonder if the spiders are watching you. Waiting.

You turn and flee the attic and then the house, taking Isabel Harcourt with you. The pernicious mist that has surrounded the place since you arrived appears to be dissipating at last. You and Isabel run down the drive, through the gates, and away down the road toward the town that lies below the cliffs.

Elijah Harcourt is gone, but the house of spiders still stands. And in its spider-haunted attic lie five corpses, a gruesome testament to the nightmarish events that befell this night.

Secret: *The House of the Dead.*

Final score: 3 stars.

The End.

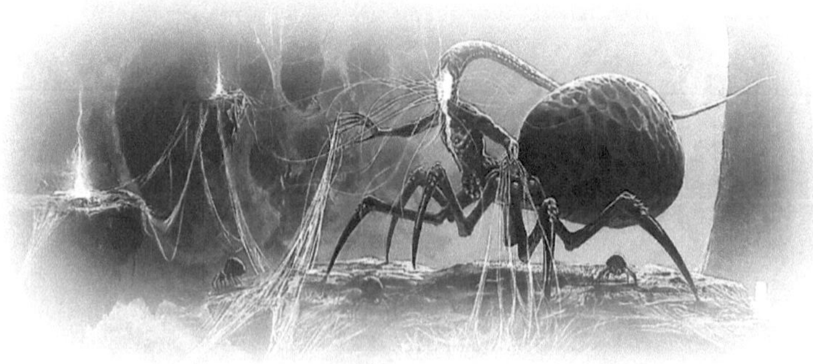

Secrets Checklist

- [ ] A Fate Worse Than Death
- [ ] A Law Unto Himself
- [ ] Above Suspicion
- [ ] Ambushed
- [ ] An Apple a Day
- [ ] Ashes to Ashes
- [ ] Behind the Bookcase
- [ ] Bite Me!
- [ ] Bookworm
- [ ] Bug Off
- [ ] Cannibalistic Humanoid Underground Dwellers
- [ ] Caught in the Web
- [ ] Creepy-Crawly
- [ ] Cut Off
- [ ] Determined
- [ ] Dutch Courage
- [ ] Eight-Legged Freaks
- [ ] Fear the Falcon
- [ ] Grim Villas in the Mist
- [ ] Hidden One
- [ ] Hidden Two
- [ ] Hidden Three
- [ ] Hidden Four
- [ ] Hidden Five
- [ ] Hidden Six
- [ ] Itsy Bitsy Spider
- [ ] Living in a Dream World
- [ ] King of Dreams
- [ ] Kiss of the Spider Woman
- [ ] Mummy's Boy
- [ ] No Lock Shall Hold Me
- [ ] Oh, What a Tangled Web
- [ ] Once Bitten
- [ ] Physician, Heal Thyself
- [ ] Poison Pen Letter
- [ ] Prime Suspect
- [ ] Secrets and Lies
- [ ] Seeing Things
- [ ] Seeker After Truth
- [ ] Spider Woman
- [ ] Spiders and Flies
- [ ] The Ash Tree
- [ ] The Butler Did It
- [ ] The Butler Didn't Do It
- [ ] The Haunting of Toby Jugg
- [ ] The House of Spiders
- [ ] The House of the Dead
- [ ] The Mists of Kingsport
- [ ] The One That Got Away
- [ ] The Ritual of Chüd
- [ ] The Spider and the Fly
- [ ] The Spiders of Leng
- [ ] The Three Amigos
- [ ] Under Suspicion
- [ ] Underhanded
- [ ] Will You Walk Into My Parlor?
- [ ] World Wide Web

Super-Secrets Checklist

☐ Finish with a combined **COMBAT + INTELLECT + WILLPOWER** of 15 or more: *Hero.*

☐ Finish with at least three stars and a combined **COMBAT + INTELLECT + WILLPOWER** of 5 or less: *A Close Call.*

☐ Finish with 2, 1 or 0 stars: *Atlach-Nacha Ascendant.*

☐ Finish the adventure using three different Investigators: *Kingsport's Protectors.*

☐ Finish with *Poison Pen Letter + Prime Suspect + The Butler Did It*: *Murder Mystery.*

☐ Finish with *Creepy-Crawly + Eight-Legged Freaks* or *Itsy Bitsy Spider*: *Dominion of the Spider God.*

☐ Finish with *Cannibalistic Humanoid Underground Dwellers + The Ritual of Chüd + World Wide Web*: *Cult of the Spider Queen.*

☐ Finish with a **SANITY** of 5 or more: *Sane.*

☐ Finish with a **HEALTH** of 5 or more: *In Fine Fettle.*

☐ Finish with a **DOOM** of 5 or more: *Doomed.*

☐ Finish with **10** or more **CLUES**: *No Stone Left Unturned.*

☐ Finish with **5** or more **RESOURCES**: *Well-prepared.*

☐ Finish with **0 CLUES**: *Lucky.*

☐ Finish with **0 RESOURCES**: *Bereft.*

☐ Finish with a **HEALTH** of **0** or below: *Like Death Warmed Up.*

☐ Finish with a **SANITY** of **0** or below: *Driven to Distraction.*

□ Finish with a **SANITY** of 0 or below, a **HEALTH** of
0 or below, and you collect all 3 Weaknesses that can
be gained in the game: *The Ultimate Price.*

□ Finish without cheating even once: *The Hard Way.*

□ Battle 4 different types of opponents: *In Self-Defense.*

□ Find *Kiss of the Spider Woman* + *The Ash Tree* +
The Haunting of Toby Jugg across several playthroughs:
Well-Read.

□ Find *Behind the Bookcase* + *Living in a Dream World*
+ *Mummy's Boy* + *The Spiders of Leng* across several
playthroughs: *The Dreamlands.*

□ Find the [**BATTERED HIP FLASK**] and
[**SILVER HIP FLASK**] in one playthrough:
Thirsty.

□ Finish with the [**FOSSIL FANG**], [**GROTESQUE
IDOL**], and [**POTTERY SHARD**]:
It Belongs in a Museum.

□ Find the [**DREAMER'S DIARY**],
[**FORGOTTEN CULTS OF HYPERBOREA**],
[**LEATHER BOOKMARK**], [**OLDE
KINGSPORT AND ITS CURIOSITIES**] and
[**THE SOMNAMBULIST'S PATH**] across
several playthroughs: *Bibliophile.*

□ Discover all 22 items across various playthroughs:
Compulsive.

□ Discover all 10 unstarred endings: *Ill-Fated.*

□ Discover all 6 *Hidden Secrets: Hunter.*

□ Discover all starred endings: *Reach for the Stars.*

□ Collect all 28 SUPER-SECRETS above this one: *Thorough.*

□ Collect all 56 in-text SECRETS: *Tireless.*

□ And if you collect both *Thorough* and *Tireless*, award
yourself *Spider Sense.*

Continuing the Adventure

If you're reading this, you have discovered that this book is part of the Investigators Gamebooks series. Therefore, once you've successfully completed any other gamebook in the series you can, if you wish, continue in a new adventure, such as this one, using your chosen Investigator. There is, of course, nothing to stop you starting fresh with a different Investigator, if you prefer.

If you do decide to continue with the same Investigator, they may gain **EXPERIENCE** based on how you fared in adventures so far. After completing an adventure, or before beginning the next one, work through the following steps to keep your Investigator up to date.

EXPERIENCE: SKILLS, HEALTH, SANITY, AND DOOM

When you complete an adventure, your Investigator's **SKILLS, HEALTH, SANITY, RESOURCES, CLUES** and **DOOM** return to their original starting values. However, roll one die for each star you earned in completing the previous adventure. In each adventure, you can earn up to four stars.

For each die which rolls a 6, you may choose one of the following:

- Increase one of your skills (**WILLPOWER, INTELLECT,** or **COMBAT**) by **+1** permanently. If any of your skills increased temporarily during the previous adventure, you should choose the skill which increased the most (if possible). Otherwise, it is your choice.
- Increase your starting **HEALTH** or **SANITY** by **+1.**
- Remove **1** starting **DOOM** from your Character Sheet.

For each die which rolls a 1, you must choose one of the following:

- Reduce one of your skills (**WILLPOWER**, **INTELLECT**, or **COMBAT**) by **-1** permanently. If any of your skills decreased temporarily during the previous adventure, you should choose the skill which decreased the most (if possible). Otherwise, it is your choice.
- Reduce your starting **HEALTH** or **SANITY** by **-1**.
- Add **1** starting **DOOM** to your Character Sheet.
- No skill may ever increase or decrease by more than **+2/-2** from your Investigator's original starting value, and no skill may decrease to lower than **1**.

HEALTH and **SANITY** may not increase to more than **10** and may not be reduced to less than **1**.

EXPERIENCE: ABILITIES AND WEAKNESSES

When you complete an adventure, you may choose one {**ABILITY**} gained during the adventure to add to your character sheet permanently. However, if you do so, you must also choose one {**WEAKNESS**} acquired during the adventure and add that to your Character Sheet permanently as well.

EXPERIENCE: ITEMS

When you complete an adventure, you may choose one [**ITEM**] gained during the adventure and add it to your Character Sheet. Other [**ITEMS**] are lost (although it's always possible you might come across the same or a similar item again in the future…). Simply put, there's only so much stuff you can carry.

RESOURCES AND CLUES

Experience does not affect **RESOURCES** or **CLUES**. Any **RESOURCES** or **CLUES** gained during the last adventure which you did not spend are lost.

Investigator

WILLPOWER

INTELLECT

COMBAT

HEALTH

Loss of Health: If your health falls below 0, you will suffer a penalty equal to it when using your combat value. So, if your health is -1, you must deduct 1 from your combat. If your health is -2, you must deduct 2 from your combat,

SANITY

Loss of Sanity: If your sanity falls below 0, you will suffer a penalty equal to it when using your willpower value. So, if your sanity is -1, you must deduct 1 from your willpower. If your sanity is -2, you must deduct 2 from your intellect, and so on.

RESOURCES

CLUES

DOOM

Items

STARTING ITEM

OTHER ITEMS

Abilities

MAJOR ABILITIES

OTHER ABILITIES

Weaknesses

MAJOR WEAKNESS

OTHER WEAKNESSES

Acknowledgments

I have long wanted to write a traditional, country house murder mystery. And while what occurred on the night of the autumnal equinox within the House of Spiders isn't a traditional, country house murder mystery, writing the adventure nonetheless scratched that particular itch.

Thanks as ever to Gwendolyn Nix and Matt Keefe at Aconyte Books, but particularly for their patience and understanding on this occasion, the franchise development team at Fantasy Flight Games, and Victor Cheng and Julian Sparrow for their meticulous playtesting.

About the Author

JONATHAN GREEN is an award-winning writer of speculative fiction, with more than eighty books to his name. He has written everything from Fighting Fantasy gamebooks to Doctor Who novels, by way of *Sonic the Hedgehog, Star Wars: The Clone Wars, Teenage Mutant Ninja Turtles*, and *Judge Dredd*. He is the creator of the Pax Britannia steampunk series for Abaddon Books, and the author of the critically acclaimed *YOU ARE THE HERO – A History of Fighting Fantasy Gamebooks*. He is currently writing his own ACE Gamebooks series, which reimagines literary classics as interactive adventures.

For Aconyte Books, he is the author of *Arkham Horror Investigators Gamebooks: The Darkness Over Arkham* and *The Tides of Innsmouth*.

ARKHAM HORROR™
INVESTIGATORS GAMEBOOKS

ARKHAM HORROR

*Prepare yourself for the terror
of the Drowned City!*

*Read the brand new prequel novels to the
Arkham Horror: The Card Game
The Drowned City expansion!*

ACONYTEBOOKS.COM
ARKHAMHORROR.COM

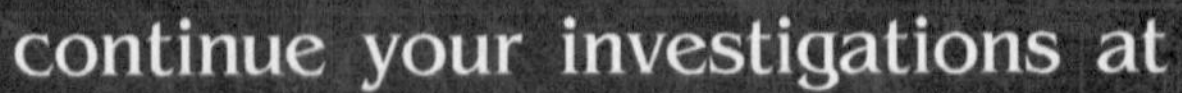

continue your investigations at

ArkhamHorror.com

Visit Arkham from the safety of your browser

Meet the
Investigators,
explore the lore,
discover your next
favourite game and
find the latest news,
all in one place

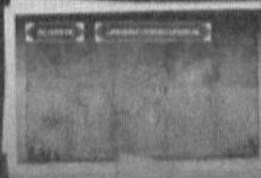

NEWS · GAMES · STORIES

LORE · FEATURES · BONUS CONTENT